"[A] captivating biography…a perceptive portrait of an artist finding herself and learning to love and paint again. Fans of Kahlo's art and of the surrealist movement will want to give this thoughtful and illuminating work a look."
—*Publishers Weekly*

"A breezy bit of art history about a 1939 affair between the author's father and Frida Kahlo in Paris…the story is transportive and dreamy." —*Kirkus Reviews*

"Marc Petitjean grew up in Paris with a haunting picture by Frida Kahlo on the walls of his family's modest apartment. Decades later, a stranger asked him about his father's love affair with Frida. This revelation, out of the blue, spurred him to investigate what had happened between them. The result is an intimate portrait, beautifully written, not only of the two lovers, but of bohemian Paris, and its most influential figures, at a turning point in history: the eve of war, in 1939. *The Heart* beats suspensefully with real life." —Judith Thurman, author of *Secrets of the Flesh: A Life of Colette*

"This book gives a poignant picture—part imagined and part true—of Frida Kahlo's days in Paris among other surrealists during a show of her paintings. It's told by the son of a French lover to whom she gave her powerful painting, *The Heart*, who was searching to understand his father better."
—Laurie Lisle, author of *Portrait of an Artist: A Biography of Georgia O'Keeffe* and *Louise Nevelson: A Passionate Life*

"In the limpid stillness of Marc Petitjean's sentences, and the focus of his gaze, *Back to Japan* becomes something deeper than a conventional biography. It's an act of profound contemplation." —Judith Thurman, author of *Secrets of the Flesh: A Life of Colette*

"A treasure of a book about a living treasure. Kunihiko Moriguchi's story is the story of Japanese craftsmanship at its most elegant, and Marc Petitjean's intimate biography is a window into a rarefied world most Japanese and foreigners never get to see." —Matt Alt, author of *Pure Invention: How Japan Made the Modern World*

"An eye-opening sojourn into the world of Japanese art and the remarkable life of a Japanese National Treasure, famed textile artist Kunihiko Moriguchi. It was a delight to read from beginning to end as well as an education into things Japanese." —Robert Whiting, author of *Tokyo Junkie*

"Kimono designer Kunihiko Moriguchi is a 'Living National Treasure,' the highest cultural recognition bestowed in Japan. But he is not simply preserving a tradition. He has absorbed a modern Western aesthetic, creating his own unique style. This is the story of how he grew up enfolded in a traditional family, learning skills from his father, then leaping into the art world of Paris in the 1960s, only to discover that his true calling lay back home in Kyoto. A rare cosmopolitan figure in the world of Japanese traditional crafts deemed worthy of Intangible Cultural Heritage status, Moriguchi is portrayed through the eyes of his French friend, filmmaker Marc Petitjean, for whom Moriguchi is a portal for understanding deep Japanese sensibilities. An intimate and engrossing portrait of an artist's life within French and Japanese culture." —Liza Dalby, author of *Geisha* and *The Tale of Murasaki*

"Through his personal interaction with the textile artist, Marc Petitjean narrates a captivating biographical story of Kunihiko Moriguchi, who is a direct successor of the long history and technique of *yūzen*, a paste-resist method of dyeing invented in the second half of the sixteenth century. Moriguchi combined Japanese tradition and Western modernity to create unique and original geometrical designs that are now his trademark. The book details his upbringing in Kyoto, his experiences in France, and influences from his mentors, such as his father and Balthus, all of which shaped who he is today as Japan's Living National Treasure. The book is a must-read for anyone who is interested in Japanese art and culture." —Yuniya Kawamura, Professor of Sociology, Fashion Institute of Technology, and author of *The Japanese Revolution in Paris Fashion*

"Marc Petitjean's wonderfully compact book delivers an intimate account of the kimono in modern times from the unique perspective of one of its most esteemed practitioners, kimono painter and Living National Treasure Kunihiko Moriguchi. More than his kimono designs, we learn about the place of the kimono and its arts in contemporary times through Moriguchi's eyes—from growing up as the son of a renowned kimono painter during the postwar poverty of Japan, escaping to Paris to find a new context for his art, and returning to Japan to define his art's own context. *Back to Japan* centers on this life-changing decision. Petitjean gives a candid portrayal of his friend and artist who fiercely protected his creative voice while proudly carrying on the artistic tradition in kimono of permanent innovation." —Vivian Li, Lupe Murchison Curator of Contemporary Art, Dallas Museum of Art, and coauthor of *Kimono Couture: The Beauty of Chiso*

"Reading this book is like overhearing someone's extraordinary story at an intimate cocktail party, with all the characters in the room, and it somehow made me nostalgic for a life before I was born—Paris in the sixties, Kyoto in the seventies. Thanks to Petitjean's sensitive observation and careful research, we get to witness the unfolding of Moriguchi's lifelong quest for creative freedom within the constraints of a traditional culture. *Back to Japan* is a real treasure." —Beth Kempton, author of *Wabi Sabi: Japanese Wisdom for a Perfectly Imperfect Life*

"Marc Petitjean takes readers on a remarkable journey into the life and art of Kunihiko Moriguchi, a Living National Treasure and one of the great masters of *yūzen*. From the galleries of Paris to the strict workshops of Kyoto, *Back to*

Japan offers an intimate glimpse of an artist who at once preserves and revolutionizes a centuries-old art form. Petitjean's poetic and heartfelt prose, along with Moriguchi's extraordinary creations, will linger in your imagination long after you close the pages." —Virginia Soenksen, Director, Madison Art Collection and Lisanby Museum, and coauthor of *Textiles of Japan*

"Marc Petitjean's *Back to Japan: The Life and Art of Master Kimono Painter Kunihiko Moriguchi* is an exquisite journey into the life trajectory and work ethos of Moriguchi. While painting a vivid portrait of the master, Petitjean also describes the eternal conflicts of modernity vs. tradition, art and artisanal thought processes, and cross-cultural otherness. This book is a rare glimpse into this rarified world and is written with sensitivity and skill." —Manami Okazaki, author of *Kimono Now*

"*Back to Japan* highlights the way art crosses borders— temporal and geographical—and weaves together friendships and family legacies. At once moving and profound, the book follows the life course of a son who, in sacrificing his own passions, discovers new modes of expression in the elegant folds and shadows of traditional yūzen dyeing. Marc Petitjean's riveting portrait of textile artist Kunihiko Moriguchi is more than biography; it is a testimony to the 'dynamic dignity' this art requires." —Rebecca Copeland, Professor of Japanese Literature, Washington University in St. Louis, and author of *The Kimono Tattoo*

A Remarkable Man

A Remarkable Man

DR. SHUNTARO HIDA

FROM HIROSHIMA TO FUKUSHIMA

Marc Petitjean

TRANSLATED FROM THE FRENCH
BY ADRIANA HUNTER

Other Press New York

Sakoda, George T., "IC099: Eleanor Roosevelt Visits the ABCC" (1953). ABCC Photograph Collection: 1946–1980. 71. https://digitalcommons.library.tmc.edu/photographs

Production editor: Yvonne E. Cárdenas
Text designer: Julie Fry
This book was set in Freight Text and Freight Sans

10 9 8 7 6 5 4 3 2 1

Library of Congress Cataloging-in-Publication Data
Names: Petitjean, Marc, author. | Hunter, Adriana, translator.
Title: A remarkable man : Dr. Shuntaro Hida from Hiroshima to Fukushima / Marc Petitjean ; translated from the French by Adriana Hunter.
Other titles: D'Hiroshima à Fukushima. English
Description: New York : Other Press, 2025. | Translation of a work originally published in 2015 as D'Hiroshima à Fukushima: Le combat du Dr Hida face aux ravages dissimulés du nucléaire by Albin Michel, Paris later revised and expanded in 2021 as Destin d'un homme remarquable: Le docteur Hida d'Hiroshima à Fukushima by Arléa, Paris.
Identifiers: LCCN 2024052606 (print) | LCCN 2024052607 (ebook) | ISBN 9781635425437 (hardcover) | ISBN 9781635425444 (ebook)
Subjects: LCSH: Hida, Shuntarō, 1917–2017—Political and social views. | Physicians—Japan—Interviews. | Hiroshima-shi (Japan)—History—Bombardment, 1945—Personal narratives. | Fukushima Nuclear Disaster, Japan, 2011—Political aspects—Japan. | Radiation—Toxicology. | Official secrets. | Japan—Relations—United States. | United States—Relations—Japan.
Classification: LCC R626.H53 A5 2025 (print) | LCC R626.H53 (ebook) | DDC 610.92 [B]—dc23/eng/20250208
LC record available at https://lccn.loc.gov/2024052606
LC ebook record available at https://lccn.loc.gov/2024052607

Secrecy, once accepted, becomes an addiction.

— EDWARD TELLER, PHYSICIST AND "FATHER" OF THE H-BOMB

CONTENTS

A Meeting

The first time I met Dr. Shuntaro Hida was in April 2005 in a Shinto cemetery, lost in the countryside some two hundred kilometers south of Tokyo. He was eighty-eight years old at the time. A very dignified figure in a suit and tie, he'd come to pay his respects to his family tomb with his wife. A letter that I'd sent him a few months earlier had been enough to persuade him to contribute to the film project *Atomic Wounds*,* which I wanted to make about the battles he'd fought. This survivor of the Hiroshima bomb, who'd been a few kilometers from the impact

---

* Which can be viewed on YouTube at https://www.youtube.com/watch?v= hIyzsN9L6ho. For more information, see http://www.marcpetitjean.fr/films /blessures-atomiques.

site at the time of the explosion, was one of the first doctors to record the sheer horror of the devastation. He was among the pioneers to suffer and catalog the appalling effects of radiation, which—in the absence of any rational explanation—was called the "Atomic Plague."* Thereafter, he spent his life treating victims of radiation; he struck me as the embodiment of an indisputable hero, someone who'd seen pure evil and stood up to it for long enough to remember what it looked like and to describe it.

I hoped that meeting him would give me access to a spiritual dimension that I felt must go hand in hand with the wisdom and humanity of such a man. But now that I was with him in that intimate moment when he was praying by his ancestors' vault, I felt out of place. He himself seemed amazed that I'd turned up in this far-flung spot with an interpreter and a camera. Even so, he came over to us with a slight smile, and said, "Rumor had it that the city of Hiroshima was completely destroyed and there were no survivors. My father went there four or five days after to find out what had happened to me, but he had no idea where I might be. He left thinking I was dead and arranged a funeral here in this village. There was no body. Imagine his emotion when I came home."

---

* *Rebel Journalism: The Writings of Wilfred Burchett*, edited by George Burchett and Nick Shimmin. Excerpt: http://assets.cambridge.org/9780521718264 /excerpt/9780521718264_excerpt.pdf.

These few words about death, disappearance, and separation paradoxically established a close and lasting tie between us. A trip to Hiroshima together, several days spent in the hospital near Tokyo where he worked, and hours of interviews at his home over the next few years allowed us to build a respectful relationship. The day before I traveled home from that first visit, he concluded our interviews by saying "Because of nuclear technology, the era that lies ahead will be far more frightening and harder to live through, but I will keep fighting." I wasn't sure what he was envisioning, but given his experience I put my faith in this prophetic pronouncement by featuring it at the end of *Blessures atomique*, which I completed in 2006. In other words, five years before Fukushima.

On March 12, 2011, following a magnitude 9.1 earthquake and a tsunami that had devastated the northeast of Japan the day before, reactor number 1 at the Fukushima nuclear plant blew up, followed two days later by reactor number 3. This plunged Japan and the rest of the world into a state of high anxiety: Fukushima was now out of control.

At the time of the explosion at the nuclear power plant, I was with friends in Kyoto, and we immediately called Dr. Hida. He wasn't surprised by the incident, merely disgusted by human stupidity, which he thought had instigated the catastrophe in a tragic, stuttering repetition of history. "You'll see," he said, "it'll be the same as Hiroshima and Chernobyl, we'll never know the true extent of the damage."

I had come to view the Japanese as a conscientious people with a strong sense of duty, and therefore naively hoped the authorities would implement effective measures to protect and help the victims. But this didn't really happen: many people were left to cope on their own and were unable to deal with the medical, economic, and human repercussions of the disaster. Following numerous demonstrations that rallied as many as sixty thousand people in Tokyo (unprecedented events in Japan, which doesn't have the same tradition as many Western countries for public expressions of opinion), the government did commit to assessing the safety of the country's fifty-four other reactors. This drew attention to the fact that some were in a state of disrepair and were in locations with a high risk of seismic activity. The state had initially stopped all reactors, but then started some up again, despite opposition from the public: the government was determined to relaunch the nuclear network.

Immediately after the disaster, civil society mobilized its response, and mothers in the Fukushima region openly expressed their fears and anger. Survivors of the Hiroshima and Nagasaki bombs, known as *hibakusha*, were valued for their firsthand experience, and were equipped to listen to these new victims, to understand them and to help them. Which is why Dr. Hida, then aged ninety-four, was in great demand to advise victims of contamination, give talks, explain the risks to the media, and secure scientific data from the authorities. I was glad to see that his reputation crossed frontiers: in January 2012, the Paris-based *Courrier international* newspaper published a three-page article about him.* With a view to continuing the work I'd started in 2005, I visited him in Tokyo, hoping that his experience of Hiroshima might help us understand how the Fukushima accident was really being handled. I kept thinking about what he'd said to me on the phone a year earlier: "You'll see, it'll be the same as Hiroshima and Chernobyl…"

Two Islands

———

Hiro-shima, "wide island," and Fuku-shima, "blessed island": Two names that conjure images of peaceful places but that now beat a macabre incantation of the history of atomic technology in contemporary Japan.

In June 2012 I accompanied the doctor when he gave a talk in Iwaki, a city some forty kilometers from the damaged power station. The audience was made up of residents and refugees from the twenty-kilometer exclusion zone. Dr. Hida's frail figure stepped onto the stage. Behind round, metal-rimmed glasses, his half-closed eyes gleamed with intelligence and humanity. He refused the chair he was offered, choosing instead to stand behind a podium to give his speech. The man who only moments before had

Dr. Hida, aged twenty-five, in 1943, when he was transferred
from the school of medicine to the military hospital in Hiroshima

looked tired as he leaned on his walking stick instantly transformed into an impassioned speaker. He used no notes. It was as if the grim events of August 6, 1945, had taken place the day before, as if only yesterday he'd stood on that hill seven kilometers from the blast before hurrying toward the pillar of fire that was Hiroshima to return to his hospital.

"My bicycle picked up speed on the little gravel trail down the hill," he said, "and I fell several times but kept going. About three kilometers from Hiroshima there was a statue of Jizo.* I had the mountain on one side and the Ota River on the other, I set off down a steep, straight incline that ended, about two hundred meters below, in a sharp bend where the path then followed the course of the river. I was just worrying about a big boulder and how steep the hillside was when something appeared suddenly, a completely black vertical outline, like a human figure, coming toward me, swaying from right to left. As it came closer, I made out a head, a face, shoulders, a body coming at me with outstretched arms, like a zombie in rags. The figure had a face but no real nose or mouth, just two lumps like bread rolls where the eyes should have been. The mouth took up the whole bottom half of the face, its lips completely retracted.

---

* Jizo is a Buddhist god who protects travelers and children. Jizo statuettes are small sculptures of a monk, carved in stone. They stand by roadsides or near temples, and are valued by the Japanese.

This thing was walking straight for me, emitting an incomprehensible noise. The more I looked, the more convinced I was that it was a human being. I was dumbstruck. I'm ashamed to admit it but I was frightened he would ask me for help. I dropped my bike and backed away. The figure quickened its pace and eventually tripped on my bike and fell. When I saw him lying there, I felt terrible and went over to help. I wanted to touch him, I needed to examine him: The things hanging from his arms weren't scraps of fabric but his skin. I tried to take his pulse, but every part of him was burnt, he had no skin left. Oh, it was so horrible! I stayed by him, trying to say encouraging things. He convulsed at my feet and then stopped moving. I didn't need to examine him to know that he was dead.

"From where I was, outside the city, I could see a huge pillar of fire, and way up at the top, a mushroom-shaped cloud. I was terrified. I realized the city was in flames. Honestly, I really wanted to turn back but I kept going toward the city. Perched on my bike, I looked along the path and saw masses of people like the ghost I'd just met, all of them burned and with outstretched arms. They were all heading in my direction. And there were so many of them. I couldn't see how I would go against the tide on my bike and get through them. The Ota River was the only possible route. I slid down a drop of seven or eight meters and waded through water up to my hips. The whole city was burning, and as I came closer, a big, black cloud spread over the surface of the river, and the violent draft from the blaze whipped the water up into my face. Charred, naked bodies fell into the river. Thousands of monsters crossed it. They walked beside me and all around me. They were coming from the far bank too. Those who were still alive moved or moaned. Cried for help. I felt I was being put to the test as a human being. If I'd let myself scream then, I would have gone mad. And it all would have been over. But on the threshold of madness…how can I put this? I resisted. I was paralyzed with fear. I didn't know what to do. I stayed there a long time before eventually accepting reality."

Dr. Hida thought the injured were bound to converge on the village of Hesaka, so he headed back there. The place was another scene of chaos: "People had to step over corpses to get into the village. I made my way to the elementary school. From the street, the schoolyard was one teeming mass of people: They'd all come to find help. The mayor, the school principal, the *bhikku* [a Buddhist monk], and the police chief all begged me to do something, anything, they were completely overwhelmed, having to watch these charred people covered in blood appearing out of nowhere with the sound of their heavy breathing. We had to anticipate tens of thousands of people in the village before nightfall. It was wartime, so there were only children and the elderly left, not a single young man. We needed to get organized. The men improvised stretchers to carry people who could no longer move to safety. The women made rice balls—it's what I'd asked them to do in the first instance, but not one of the survivors was in any state to eat a rice ball. Their hands were burned. And their faces. So we put all the balls into a cooking pot to make a pulp. Two young girls carried the pot, and a boy fed the people lying on the ground. That was what I did first.

"I was frightened. Terribly frightened. When a patient dies in the hospital, you have time to prepare for it, you can estimate how long they have left to live. Family members can gather around the sickbed to say goodbye and pay their respects. But this was completely different. People were dying without even knowing why. I knelt beside them, and they looked into my eyes so penetratingly! I guess they wanted to ask what was happening to them, but they couldn't utter a single word. They were in pain and pleading for help. Their eyes spoke with such intensity that I'll never forget the way they looked at me. I could see resentment in them. They were blaming me for still being able-bodied. They held me accountable. They thought it was unfair. Eyes full of regret and hate. I was obsessed by the look in all those eyes in their dying moments. I desperately wanted to run away from those terrifying eyes, but I had nowhere to go—they followed me everywhere. I was watching people die, and that's a horrifying situation for a doctor.

"Three days after the explosion, on the morning of August 9, 1945, military doctors, nurses, and nurse's aides came to the village from the Kyushu and Shikoku regions, bringing medication and medical equipment. There were more than a hundred of them. It was early in the morning; the villagers and I were still asleep. One of the nurses called out to me, concerned that all the patients had temperatures above 104 degrees Fahrenheit. That was unusual in general medicine. This intrigued me, and I then studied each patient closely. Some of them had symptoms I'd never seen. Their noses, mouths, and eyes were bleeding. I'd never known anyone's eyes to bleed. I needed to examine them, but the smell coming from them was intolerable. The fact is their mouths were decomposing. I suspected inflammation in their tonsils. They were all lying on their side, the only position that was just about bearable for them, and I knelt to examine them. I asked them to turn to roll onto their backs to face me so that I could examine their mouths, but they couldn't do even that. They weren't being uncooperative; they just couldn't do it. So I lay down beside them so that I was facing them and tried to open their mouths with a small spoon. The throat is usually dark pink, and it becomes red when you're sick. But that's not what I saw. Their throats were completely black. As if they'd been forced to swallow India ink. But I couldn't stay lying like that for long, because the smell was so appalling. I realized their flesh was decomposing. Everyone knows the human body decomposes after death, but these people were still alive. None of it made any sense. I overcame my disgust and continued to examine them.

"Another thing: I said they were burned all over, but some parts of their bodies, such as the insides of their arms, weren't burned. And yet these areas hurt too, and I noticed they were dotted with purpura, purple patches, twenty or thirty of them, they looked like the marks left by an ink stamp. A professor at med school had told me about a rare pathology that we would probably never see, and one of its symptoms was purpura: it was a blood disorder that at the time gave the sufferer a life expectancy of two or three days. As I looked at other patients, I noticed the same purpura in all of them. Something very strange was going on. There they were, dying. They were lying there, waiting for the end, and they couldn't help touching their hair, which fell out easily. Despite the state they were in, the women demonstrated their distress by brandishing handfuls of hair. No disease could cause such radical hair loss from just stroking your own head. I didn't understand at all. Last, they were suffering pulmonary hemorrhages: blood was infiltrating the alveoli at the ends of their airways, and, unable to breathe, they ended up hawking up blood, which literally jetted from their mouths, arcing sometimes two or three meters above the ground where they lay. I was in danger of being showered with blood at any moment. That's how the radiation victims died; it's called acute radiation syndrome. It was caused by very powerful external radiation that penetrated their bodies and destroyed their cells.

"We'd gathered together more than thirty thousand injured in that village of about one hundred inhabitants. We were short of space, it was such chaos! I was examining a patient on the ground when someone tugged insistently at my jacket sleeve: it was a uniformed soldier with no obvious injuries, and he told me he hadn't been a victim of the bomb. I was there working without a break from morning till night and I unceremoniously sent him packing, saying he had no business there if he hadn't been affected by the bomb. He left. Three days later, someone else died on the same spot, and I remembered the soldier and asked people if they knew what had happened to him. They said he'd died, like everyone else. But he hadn't arrived in Hiroshima until midday on the day of the explosion, which had been at eight fifteen. He and other soldiers from a garrison fifty kilometers away had helped inhabitants all through the night, on into the morning and the next few days, until he lost consciousness on August 9. He wasn't the only case like this. Other people who'd gone to look for family members one or two days after the explosion eventually started to feel that their bodies were unbearably heavy, and they were unable to stay on their feet. Still others, people from, say, Osaka or Kyushu, came to Hiroshima in the week after the bombing. In the space of a month, I saw huge numbers of people suffering like this. I had no idea what was happening to them, but my experience told me they had something in common. I now know that these people hadn't been directly exposed to 'external' radiation: They'd reached the city *after* the bomb exploded and ingested radioactivity without realizing it, by breathing the air, drinking the water, or eating tomatoes or cucumbers picked in the fields. That's what's known as internal radiation."*

Of course, at the time, nothing was known about such residual radiation, and in the case of Fukushima, the responsible parties are still behaving as if it doesn't pose any danger. Which is how Professor Yamashita, who advised on managing the nuclear risks at Fukushima, was able to make this astonishing announcement: "You won't risk anything by smiling.

---

* There are two distinct types of exposure to radiation: external radiation, when a radioactive source irradiates the whole body or an organ from the outside, and internal contamination, which occurs when radionuclides are ingested or inhaled.

Internal radiation is ten times less dangerous than external." Some scientists and leading figures in the nuclear industry even said that a good dose of radio-activity was beneficial to the organism (the potential positive effects of small doses is called hormesis). These were the sort of absurdities that people who'd come to listen to the doctor that afternoon had been subjected to all day long for months on the radio and television. But Dr. Hida addressed them with stagger-ing candor: "Most of you are bound to have absorbed radioactive particles after the accident. I don't think it's possible to avoid and I'm afraid the real problems are still to come. Our government doesn't have a good grasp of the subject and is proving incapable of properly informing the public. In a few years, I antic-ipate seeing the same diseases as in Hiroshima and Nagasaki. It's insanity to say there are no grounds for concern. Quite the opposite, this is just the begin-ning. Does that mean all of you will get sick and die? The answer to that is no. But it gives you an increased risk of leukemia, all sorts of cancers, and cardiac complaints—I know that's not easy to hear. Maybe you won't have these problems, but maybe you will."

Dr. Hida's defiance toward the public authorities has its origins in his experiences tending the hibakusha. Over the course of sixty years he examined some six thousand patients, two-thirds of whom hadn't been at the site at the time of the explosion but who had gone there later or had even stayed relatively far away. In some cases, the symptoms appeared ten or twenty years later, sometimes more than thirty years later. He was convinced that these contaminations were due to radioactive dust, which had risen to an altitude of more than ten thousand meters before dropping back down and spreading all over Japan. He attributed the malicious hypocrisy of the Japanese state's advice to declarations made by the United States after the explosion, saying "The first American soldiers arrived on Japanese soil on September 2, 1945, so just under a month after the atomic bombing. They told the populations of Hiroshima and Nagasaki: 'If you were not present on the days of the bombings because you were in Osaka and Fukuoka, if you arrived at the city later to look for your children and your wife in the wreckage over the following days, and some of you fell gravely ill, know that this illness has nothing to do with the atomic bomb.' The U.S. Army, which had developed the bomb, gave assurances that levels of internal radiation were so low that they had no effect on health. A little later, still in September 1945, they stated that 'All those who were going to die as a result of radioactivity from the atomic explosion are already dead, and we no longer observe any physiological impact from residual radiation.' These statements were made not only to the

Japanese population but also to the whole world via the UN. The U.S. Army made the most of its authority over the Japanese during the occupation to make these declarations after its new bomb had been used for the first time. And the Japanese believed them!"

In the six weeks before the U.S. Army's occupation of Hiroshima, eighteen teams of Japanese radiologists and other scientists, more than two thousand people, went to the site and gathered large amounts of data and statistics related to the bomb's effects on its victims. They collected irradiated organs and substances and wrote thirty-four reports. All this material, along with films and photos taken at the time, was requisitioned and—mostly—sent to Washington. The occupiers also appropriated compilations of data as well as systems for gathering information and samples. Furthermore, the army implemented censorship. Until 1951, the Japanese were banned from publishing articles about the bomb and its consequences. This is one reason why it took so long for Dr. Hida to understand what had caused his patients' conditions: "When General Douglas MacArthur came to Japan, he announced that he was now the country's governor, and the Japanese population was under his orders. He also drew up a list of everything we weren't allowed to do, including one particular ban that as a doctor I found unacceptable: He said that the atomic bomb was an American weapon classified as a defense secret, which meant that all information relating to the atomic bomb was protected. This included the effects of radioactivity on victims. Many survivors were injured or had sustained burns, and MacArthur ordered these victims to view their symptoms as 'defense secrets.' He forbade them to discuss them even with their families. Japanese doctors and researchers were given instructions: victims could consult a doctor, but no medical notes could be kept. No written record. We weren't allowed to conduct studies at the Academy of Medicine. Working with other doctors using the data that had been gathered was also banned. Any sort of research was banned. Doctors could no longer practice properly. It was a complete brick wall. At the time, we couldn't discuss the subject under any circumstances. We couldn't even refer to it. MacArthur made it clear that anyone who infringed these bans would be severely punished by the Allied forces. We were overseen by armed soldiers and definitely didn't want to attract their attention, so we kept quiet.

"Doctors in Hiroshima who were lucky enough to survive did everything they could to treat the victims. American guards kept an eye on their work, and any doctors who attracted more patients than others became subject to close monitoring. The soldiers even went into doctors' offices to watch how they examined their patients and recorded their findings.

Once these documents had been studied, the doctors were judged individually. The military advised the Japanese Academy of Medicine, which in turn sent out warnings to the doctors concerned. Under pressure like this, doctors eventually backed down. I was given warnings myself. The United States wanted to do everything it could to hide the facts about the damage caused by the A-bomb—particularly the effects of internal radioactivity. They didn't want the whole world to find out the truth: confronted with such a multiplicity of similar cases, theories about the effects of residual radiation were becoming a serious issue. Other doctors were taking an interest in the subject, studies would be published, and would raise international awareness. This might threaten the civil nuclear power program that the United States intended to develop and export. The United States was afraid it would come to that."

Proof of the existence and dangers of internal radiation could, at any moment, ruin the technological, industrial, and commercial progress that the Americans were starting to make with the atom. It was a secret, one to be kept hidden even from the military. The fact was that by dropping an atomic bomb on the enemy three thousand kilometers away, a country ran the risk of being landed with radioactive fallout itself and contaminating its own population, its fields, and its water table. All it took was a gust of wind. Better not to mention the fallout. It didn't exist or it had no effect on health. This communications strategy was used successfully for nearly seventy years—the French may remember that the "Chernobyl cloud" allegedly stopped at the French frontier, while the Germans had banned drinking milk because grazing land was contaminated. The same communication strategy was used with Fukushima.

Since 1993, the Nuclear Safety Department of the Japanese Ministry of Education, Sports, Science, and Technology has implemented SPEEDI (System for Prediction of Environmental Emergency Dose Information) as a way of rapidly alerting the population in instances of radioactive pollution. But the data gathered after the Fukushima explosion on March 11, 2011, although transmitted almost immediately to the U.S. Army, was not made public in Japan until two weeks later. What's more, the measurements recorded between March 11 and 15 that would have allowed the population to evacuate the most highly contaminated areas straightaway were "accidentally" erased. Truth be told, this data wasn't made public because the figures were so high that the authorities thought they'd been measured incorrectly. A map of contamination across Japan was circulated, then swiftly altered. There was no point unnecessarily panicking the population. Neither should they give credence to the idea that radioactive pollution could spread hundreds of kilometers from the site, as it had with Hiroshima and Nagasaki. The Japanese government was prepared to do anything to prove that radioactivity was innocuous; one politician, Yasuhiro Sonoda, even went so far as to be filmed drinking water from a nuclear reactor cooler.*

After Dr. Hida's speech, the audience was invited to ask questions. One young woman with a child in her arms spoke up: "Fukushima's an agricultural region. We eat what we grow on our land, but mothers in Fukushima now have to buy vegetables from other sources, on the internet or through support networks. After such a serious accident, I'm sure eating local produce is a health risk. I can't even envision serving it in canteens. They say our vegetables are no threat, they're not dangerous. How stupid do they think we are?"

In the early weeks after the disaster, the authorities announced unequivocally that the provenance of foodstuffs would be subject to labeling, but consumers very soon found radioactive foodstuffs—rice, tea, and vegetables—in the south of the country, when Fukushima is in the north. It was also clear that irradiated cattle from Fukushima had been transported

---

* Justin McCurry, *The Guardian*, November 1, 2011.

to other regions: the government's idea was to share the risk of contamination across the whole population and support the flagging regional economy. Questions of public health were obviously not a priority. Some individuals benefited from the situation, such as the meat wholesaler in Osaka who sold fifteen hundred kilos of beef labeled as being from Kagoshima (a prefecture in the southernmost tip of the country) when it actually came from Fukushima or its region, Tohoku. He justified his actions by saying it was hard to sell products labeled "Made in Fukushima."

On the drive back to Tokyo, it rained copiously. Squalls of wind buffeted the trees and smacked against the car windows. I pictured the radioactive particles inside the raindrops, their journey down the tall trees, over the ground, into the earth, and onto vegetables; and I thought about *kami*, the spirits of Shinto, the traditional shamanic religion of Japan. They personify natural phenomena: rivers, trees, mountains, and rocks. I was wondering how the *kami* lived alongside atomic particles when Dr. Hida's voice roused me from my musing: "Last week a case was reported to me of a woman in Minamisoma, near Fukushima, who ended up hiding her symptoms. She was worried because her hair started falling out. She didn't dare go out without covering her head and began talking to friends about it. Eventually, everyone knew her story. But the local authorities claimed that everything was fine, so people, neighbors, started telling her to keep quiet and not spread panic. That's a true story."

The doctor was always on the lookout, ready to fight and speak out against injustice. I pointed this out to him, and he replied with a laugh, saying he was following in the footsteps of his samurai ancestors. His past was still a relative mystery to me. He'd refused to talk about his private life and family, saying that only his fight against nuclear radiation mattered. There are many causes for his anger—from the use of the atomic bomb to military censorship—but of them all, the question of the survivors' dignity is particularly sensitive: "The bomb was dropped toward the end of the war. The Americans obviously had a specific objective, and I focused a lot on that. I took a very close interest, gathering information and meeting people, and I came to these conclusions: first of all, it was a demonstration of strength, a sort of military dissuasion tactic aimed at the Soviet Union. Showing that they were the mightiest. And second, it was a life-size trial to measure the atomic bomb's impact on structures and living things. For example, measuring the range of the radiation, the force of the explosion, and the heat. They needed to blow up the bomb so that they could analyze all these elements together. I'll tell you what I'm basing these ideas on:

first, the time that the bomb was dropped—eight fifteen. It was calculated; the U.S. Army had studied life in Hiroshima. Over the previous few days, they'd flown over the city several times taking photos. They chose eight fifteen because most Japanese were out of doors then, for example in the city's schools, where children would line up before filing into their classrooms, or the local army barracks, where soldiers exercised in their yard at this time of day. It was carefully analyzed. And what's more, they implemented the ABCC* straight after the bombings to study the effects of radioactivity on the human body. They had it all planned."

President Truman founded the scientific committee, the ABCC, in 1946. A first team would start work in the heart of the destroyed city the following year, and then, in 1950, the organization moved into state-of-the-art premises overlooking Hiroshima, well away from the radiation. People called the building the Fishcake because of its rounded shape. While American doctors and researchers worked there setting up and running a number of different programs, quantities of Japanese employees were recruited for day-to-day tasks, home visits, and biological testing.

---

* Atomic Bomb Casualty Commission. A recommended book on the subject is M. Susan Lindee's *Suffering Made Real*, University of Chicago, 1994.

"The city was destroyed. The Americans came along and put up this spanking new building on Hiji-yama hill. A real palace, in our eyes. It wasn't tall, it was a single-story semicircular building. It was beautiful. Not unlike a hospital, with the smell of disinfectant, the medical equipment, the nurses in white coats—it's hardly surprising that everyone thought they'd be treated there. A lot of hibakusha were in a bad way, and they went there without appointments. But instead of being treated, they were examined and studied like guinea pigs. The American government had given orders not to tend to the hibakusha's wounds or treat their conditions because they didn't want anyone thinking they regretted what they'd done or were apologizing for using the bomb. In the early months, the staff were friendly and gave chewing gum to children, but the survivors were reticent, particularly the women, because they had to undress in front of soldiers. The staff couldn't care less about these qualms and stripped them naked, not giving them a shred of dignity. So people refused to go there, and the hospital emptied of victims. The management had all their contact details and ended up sending out jeeps to collect patients from wherever they were, in ruined buildings or shacks. And that's how the hospital filled up again. People who were ill as a result of internal contamination went there as a last resort, having run out of ideas for how to get better. A few times I accompanied them in groups of three or four, sometimes in a little cart.

"When hibakusha arrived, they took off their dirty clothes, they were disinfected with DDT, and they put on white gowns handed out by the center. Nurses examined external symptoms—burns and wounds—and hospitalized the patients, then proceeded to do all sorts of investigations, took blood samples, and analyzed their urine and stools. They took biopsies of damaged flesh to be examined under the microscope. The tissue was frozen to make it easier to work with: they could then slice it into very thin samples. There were no operational laboratories in Japanese universities at the time, so this tissue was flown to the United States. And the patients were sent home. That was how the center worked in the early days. But before patients were admitted, they had to answer a raft of questions: Where were you at eight fifteen on the morning of the bombing? What were the circumstances of your exposure to the bomb? And so on. If the victim—who might be sick because they'd absorbed radioactive particles—replied that they hadn't been in Hiroshima at the time of the explosion but three days later, the nurse would tell them that only people who'd been directly exposed to the bomb were being treated, and so they were free to go home. I witnessed several instances like this. So I can state for sure that the ABCC ran no studies on internal radiation. The center's researchers were in contact with residual radiation themselves. It was everywhere, on food, on everyday items and most of all on the victims' bodies. But no one realized it was dangerous. Only a handful of researchers understood the real danger, for example, the Department of Biology and Medicine at the Manhattan Project.* It was a well-kept secret. The center's primary objective was to find an effective treatment for American soldiers who might be directly exposed to an atom bomb in another war."

A brochure published by the ABCC in 1951 states that the center had up to 1,000 employees, 920 of whom were Japanese. Between 1947 and 1950, 120,000 survivors were examined, providing the raw material for research into genetics, leukemia, cancers, sterility, and aging. The results of the ABCC's studies, which could have helped Japanese doctors treat hibakusha, were never made public. For many years, the ABCC simply published reports stating that the bombs hadn't caused malformations in the victims' descendants.

I was so shocked by what the doctor told me that I undertook research to corroborate his account. It was during this process that, in the ABCC archives at the library of the Texas Medical Center and the

---

* The American research project that produced the first atomic bomb.

Houston Academy of Medicine, I came across correspondence from James Neel, the leading geneticist who had headed up the studies.

Every aspect of the work was thoroughly documented with photographs: X-ray rooms, biological analysis labs, wards, and how adult and child "patients" were handled during their examinations. The hibakusha forced smiles for the camera, but their distress is obvious. Some victims were photographed like ex-convicts, stripped to the waist and holding a sign giving the date and place. All the photos were taken with a flash, which gives them a cold, clinical, and totally dehumanizing quality and confirmed that the bomb victims were treated as objects for observation. One batch of photos was devoted to specific events: during the 1950s the ABCC site became a tourist attraction, a cabinet of curiosities visited by journalists and personalities such as Marilyn Monroe and her husband at the time, Joe DiMaggio. Princess Chichibu (wife of the Japanese emperor's eldest younger brother) and other members of the Japanese imperial family made the trip several times. When Mrs. Roosevelt visited, she launched a major debate about the fact that the victims weren't being treated, but it didn't change anything. She looks displeased in one of the images.

Other photos were of autopsies, one of the topics described by Dr. Hida: "We lost everything because of

During a visit to the ABCC in 1953, Eleanor Roosevelt attends
an assembly and confers with ABCC director Grant Taylor.

the bomb, we didn't know where to sleep and we had nothing to eat. So the ABCC recruited survivors with the promise that they'd be fed. They were strictly forbidden to discuss what they'd seen and done at the center, on pain of death. The Japanese police force was virtually nonexistent. You could be beaten to death by an American soldier, and he would go unpunished. The Japanese were treated worse than cattle. The threat was serious, no one wanted to risk their life. But after a few glasses of sake…some people talked. That's how I found out they were doing autopsies.

"Some patients died at the center, and the researchers then dissected them, cutting up everything, the brain, the organs. They put it all into jars filled with formalin and sent it to the United States. After the dissection there was nothing left but skin and bone, so they stuffed the bodies with straw, hurriedly stitched their bellies together, and returned them to their families like that. With more and more bodies to process, they couldn't stuff them all. They stopped even bothering to make the deceased look presentable, they'd return just a thumb to the family and explain that the rest had been incinerated."

A few years later, the hibakusha demonstrated for the restitution of these bodies, or what was left of them, so that they could be incinerated in temples in keeping with Japanese tradition. In May 1973, the U.S. Army's Institute of Pathology eventually returned job lots of organs in large jars, along with autopsy reports and photos. But there was nothing to prove that these really were the remains of victims of the bomb. Some of these remains are still kept at the Atomic Bomb Disease Institute at the University of Nagasaki.

The ABCC was transferred to the Japanese in 1975 under the name the Radiation Effects Research Foundation (RERF), still under the supervision of American scientists. The RERF did little to help the population after the Fukushima accident.

———

June 2013. I'm strolling around Tokyo's Shinjuku quarter, waiting to meet friends. Passersby go in and out of subway stations and department stores. Do they ever think about the radioactive contamination all around them? My Japanese friends arrive and pick a restaurant. Will they ask the waiter about the provenance of the ingredients of our meal? They laugh out loud at the question: "Never! You can't know everything, so we'd rather not think about it and have a good time. It won't kill us."

I feel instantly ashamed of my caution. They live here year-round, and the visiting foreigner that I am is suggesting they're in danger. During the meal, I pass on sushi—which I love—and settle for chicken skewers. I can see there's no logic to my choice: Who said chicken was safe from contamination? I can only imagine the conundrum this poses for people who live here. It's not even easy to contemplate waking every morning thinking about possible radioactivity.

The contamination from Hiroshima and Nagasaki originated from one-off incidents: the bombs. Although, of course, the effects were spread over several months, even a year, however long it took for the black rain and fallout to be drained out to sea by the rain. But with Fukushima the contamination is continuous and has comprehensively impregnated the environment. "Living with it" is the notion that Dr. Hida dreads along with the imminent prospect of Fukushima's victims.

"The greatest fear that hibakusha have to live with is the threat of cancer. They can't plan ahead like everyone else. When we go to school, when we get married…we're constantly faced with this fear. Our basic rights have been stolen, and we live with the certainty that we'll inevitably develop a condition as a result of our exposure to the atomic bomb. But we don't know exactly when it will happen, so we live in fear. Even though we do get money from the state as compensation, that doesn't resolve anything. Money can't repay the sixty-three years I've suffered."

The public authorities in Fukushima are investing extensively in erasing traces of radionuclides in the

Japanese countryside. They've embarked on depolluting the most-exposed places, particularly schools. But there's a shortage of storage sites: in some cases, highly radioactive waste is packed under tarpaulins in the corner of the schoolyard. If the locals protest, the waste is moved in anticipation of a hypothetical new destination. The same goes for waste in towns submerged by the tsunami that were polluted by radioactive fallout. It's a way of gently increasing background levels of radioactivity around the country: this dissemination into the environment will cause what could be called a "better spread" of health complaints in the future, embracing the whole Japanese territory. It will therefore be easier to deny that the Fukushima region was worse affected than others, and by extension to claim that overall a nuclear accident isn't all that catastrophic. Local governments will burn their radioactive waste, and the wind will carry the ash to other parts of the country…

Living for Other People

———

After Hiroshima, Dr. Hida traveled across Japan and many other countries to talk about his experiences and the diseases and suffering of the hibakusha. His own obvious good health meant people almost forgot that he, too, had been irradiated. In the space of a day, he might have meetings with journalists, antinuclear campaigners, and hibakusha, as well as giving talks and carrying out consultations at the hospital. When I first met him, I was struck by his calm and determination. In 2016, at nearly 100 years old, he still looked in excellent health. Some people who met him at conferences or symposia, in schools or television studios were amused by this apparent contradiction: "Looks like radiation's a good preservative!"

While others saw him as chosen by God and asked, "How come you didn't die along with the others?" He has a simple answer to this question: "We were all irradiated at the same location, some died and others didn't. The quantity of radiation an individual is exposed to has absolutely no influence over their reaction. Some have good enough resistance; it varies from one person to another. I wasn't directly exposed to the radiation, but I breathed contaminated air and drank huge amounts of water in that devastated city because the sun beat down relentlessly while I was working among the ruins: water spouted from broken pipes, and I drank it. I must have ingested substantial doses of radioactivity like that.

"A week after the explosion, I started to feel very tired, I was cold and feverish, as if I'd caught a cold. I'm usually quite energetic and quick off the mark. The military doctors who'd come to provide backup often needed me because they didn't know the neighborhood, so I always had people around me. They noticed the change in my behavior and were worried. At that point, we thought the victims had a contagious disease, a sort of epidemic, and that I'd caught it. We had to act quickly because people were dying. The fact that they had purpuras, the purplish blotches on their skin, could imply a blood disorder, so we had to find compatible blood and do transfusions. We ran blood group tests on young soldiers and nurses who hadn't been irradiated, for example people from Kyushu, to find a compatible donor. The methods at the time were nothing like those we have now: we didn't do transfusions of between three hundred and five hundred milliliters back then, instead we gave injections of twenty milliliters of blood every day for about a week. It's true: I did feel better afterward. My coworker would catch me every morning before I went to work to give me a transfusion. They were doing everything they could for me: I was the only doctor from Hiroshima, and I knew the city. They really saved my life."

In fact, there were 298 doctors listed in the city at the time of the explosion. Sixty of them were killed instantly and twenty-eight helped victims, whose numbers are estimated at more than a hundred thousand.

"In the long term, radiation accelerates the aging process. As a result, my bones have aged very quickly, and my back's always been in a terrible state. At its worst, I was in so much pain I had to drag myself along the ground. In the end, I had no choice but to have an operation when I was sixty-one. Everything was pretty much fine for ten years after the operation, but my condition got worse when I was seventy, and I was hospitalized again. I couldn't be operated on in the same place, so they injected painkillers into my spinal cord. I held out another ten years, until I was eighty, but I walked with a stick, it wasn't a pretty sight. I'd come around to the idea of retiring from all my work, I'd even written letters of resignation to the hospital and the doctor's office where I worked. I'd tried everything, every treatment known to surgery and different medication, as well as acupuncture and moxibustion.*

"The only form of therapy I hadn't yet tried was walking in water. There was a swimming pool just two hundred meters from our house, and my wife took me there in a wheelchair. Once inside the building, I got about by leaning on her shoulder and managed to walk after a fashion. The pool had only just been opened, and there weren't many people there. As you know, the body feels lighter in water. I managed to stand on my own with only a little trouble, when I was usually in a lot of pain when I tried to get up or stay standing. I attempted one step forward and succeeded. And so I did lengths like that, slowly and resolutely. Twenty trips up and down and I would already have traveled a kilometer. I didn't have any pain, I could walk. But the minute I got out of the water, I was in terrible pain, just like before. Back at home, I rested contentedly, happy with how I'd felt in the water, and I decided to go back every day and keep

---

* A technique, similar to acupuncture, in which burning, dried mugwort is applied to points on the body.

a note of my progress. Day after day I went farther. I set myself a goal to walk the distance from Tokyo to Hiroshima in the pool, that's nine hundred kilometers. It would take nine hundred days, or about three years. I persevered, and after the first eight months the pain had gone. So I managed to get all the way to Hiroshima without my walking stick!

"Nowadays I sometimes get a heavy feeling in my lumbar spine. It's to be expected, I'm getting old. But it doesn't stop me living my life. It's been eighteen years already. And walking in water has had other health benefits: I've gotten younger! I'm a grandpa, I should have wrinkles, but because of pool walking, my skin's stayed smooth. No wrinkles. After my recovery, I gradually returned to work. At eighty you can definitely want to stop working, it's even considered socially normal. But this feeling was stronger than I am: I couldn't resign myself to stopping work. The bomb victims rely on me. They need to see me and talk to me."

In the Shinto faith, blood is considered impure, so people have to purify themselves with water for fear of being cursed. Every temple has an area devoted to purification with a *chozuya* or *temizuya*—stone basins in which the faithful can cleanse their hands and mouths by following a precise ritual, using a wooden or copper ladle. Had Dr. Hida's wading along the Ota River played a purifying role for his body, considering what it had undergone in the hours after the explosion? I asked him whether, at what had been a time of extreme distress, he'd turned to prayer or rituals from Shintoism, Buddhism, or another faith in his efforts to withstand or transcend the ordeal. He told me that he'd simply focused on the realities before him: tending, reassuring, and understanding. But once the first horror was past, he'd wondered what meaning he could now ascribe to his own life and to the world. A survivor, but what for? Who for?

"I survived when so many died. I gradually started to believe that my life surely had some particular meaning: I must live for the people who left me before their time. I must nurture my own life, become a doctor to serve the people, and live as long as possible. This sense of duty, which has always guided me through difficult times, has meant I've kept going this far. Whatever the situation, so long as I'm still alive, my life has a meaning: making myself useful to others. So I need to look after it and never forget to live every moment to the full. That really means a lot to me."

It took many years to formulate how he could help other people. This path that made him a universal humanist did not take him via religion or spirituality, as many might expect, but via materialism. The hibakusha were in pain: he treated them and brought their lives to the attention of the world; of Japanese society, which excluded them; and the Japanese state, which did too little for them too late. Medicine and social justice are linked. For hibakusha the war didn't end on August 15, 1945, as it did for other Japanese nationals. They suffered the physical and psychological effects of the atomic bomb for decades, and this suffering was passed on to the second and third generations. The bomb didn't cause damage only at the time of the explosion, as the Americans claimed; it ruined the lives of hundreds of thousands of people. And if by the mid-2010s the Japanese and American governments did officially recognize this truth, then they effectively also recognized the danger of internal radiation for the inhabitants of Fukushima. This was the point that Dr. Hida argued.

Once the U.S. Army had drawn up and implemented a new constitution for Japan, one of the missions that it set itself was to democratize this society currently living under an imperial regime. Dr. Hida's experience of this capitulation is characteristic of the Japanese mindset of the period, which left no room for individualism: "The emperor announced the end of the war on the radio on August 15. I remember that the head of the hospital and the principal of the school where we were based wore ceremonial clothing that morning. And the soldiers their decorations. We listened to the emperor's speech, but it wasn't easy: there was so much noise. Despite this, I could tell from his tone of voice that the war had just ended; I'd already guessed as much when the head of the hospital told me to put on my formal clothes, and I'd been worried that he would decide to take his own life. He was a very conscientious man. If he'd done that, I would have had no choice but to follow him. So I carried a firearm in case I had to die, because I had absolutely no desire to kill myself with a saber—it's incredibly painful, slicing your own stomach open! The boss told me not to do anything rash. He told me to calm down, there would be no collective suicide. But I had genuinely prepared for my possible hara-kiri…True to tradition, I'd put the white belt around my waist, and I carried a saber and a pistol to hasten the end. I hated the army, but I was a soldier all the same, and therefore ready to die a worthy death if my boss asked it of me. I couldn't be found lacking if the people I worked with chose to die."

In December 1945, on the orders of the occupying forces, the Japanese regime voted in a law that required all organizations and companies in whatever field to have unions. At the time, Dr. Hida worked in a hospital in the Hiroshima region.

"One day the hospital director summoned all the managers. 'I have no idea how a union works,' he told us. 'Can anyone enlighten me?' I was the only person at Yanaï Hospital who vaguely knew what a union was, so I was nominated president and tasked to set one up. Many of the elected leaders in other regions had been active in clandestine movements during the war or had been militant communists. We were all invited to a meeting at the headquarters in Tokyo. I had family there, so I was chosen as the region's delegate. The Daiichi Byôin National Hospital had been built on the site of the former military school of medicine. It had a sort of cabin on its roof, and that's where the national headquarters was established and where I met my fellow organizers. They were very surprised to see a doctor show up; the others were nurses, secretaries, or cooks. I spent my time there with the president, who'd been in the resistance during the war. We visited all the national hospitals in Tokyo and the surrounding area. It felt like intensive training in trade unionism. In the end, they didn't want me to leave and elected me as the organization's vice president."

In the immediate aftermath of the war, Japan was exhausted. Of its overall population of seventy-two million, twenty-two million were homeless. People had nothing to eat and wandered the streets and the countryside looking for anything that would pass as food. The supply chain to Tokyo had broken down, and the population demanded rice and then started looting shops. On April 7, 1946, during a riot that had brought fifty thousand people to the prime minister's residence, the police fired at the crowd and asked the American military for backup. Nearly a month later, on May 1, two million people joined anti-government demonstrations with cries of "Down with the emperor!"

"The national hospitals were state-run, overseen by the minister for health and social affairs. But life had gotten complicated for civil servants after the reforms and with the new laws. In September 1946, civil servants demonstrated against other employees who were demanding a pay raise. We were determined: all civil servants would strike. It was the first big social movement after the war. At the last minute, the very day before the strike, the occupying army intervened and General MacArthur forbade the strike. Li Yashiro, the powerful president of the national railway company's union, was choked with emotion when he announced on the radio that the strike had been abandoned. I personally had been right in the thick of this social movement at a national level, so I'd inevitably attracted the attention of the authorities, who took exception to my commitment to victims of the atomic bombs. My every action was monitored day and night. I was on the occupiers' blacklist."

Against this explosive backdrop, Dr. Hida tended to people injured in the demonstrations and continued to look for solutions to treat the hibakusha.

"We were struggling to find the cause of the symptoms observed in the atomic bomb victims. At the time we had no idea what internal radiation was. Not one university professor could explain it. I had only one solution left: to ask the Americans themselves for explanations. I often met the health minister in my role as vice president of the hospital unions. I knew him well. In 1948 I told him this was a question of survival for the Japanese people, the war was over and he must go see General MacArthur in person and demand all the documents that detailed the effects of radioactivity that had been seized from the Japanese. And ask him to tell us what the ABCC's doctors and scientists knew about the conditions caused by radioactivity. I took the opportunity to give him this message myself at a meeting between the government and the union. He told me I was crazy and said, 'General MacArthur doesn't even give the emperor permission to visit him, so he'll never agree to see a mere Japanese health minister.' He had no intention of going, so I said, 'You're the last hope, the guarantor for the health of the Japanese people. This is a matter of life and death. It's your responsibility to go see him in the name of all the Japanese, even if it costs you your life.' Outraged by this, he challenged me: 'If you feel so strongly about it, you should just go yourself!' I asked him if he was serious, and he said he couldn't see any harm in my going if it was really necessary. I said I'd go the very next day."

———

June 2013: Dr. Hida and I went to the building in which the U.S. Army had set up its headquarters, looking out at the emperor's palace and its park in the center of Tokyo; it was now the head office of the Dai-ichi Seimei insurance company and was called DN Tower 21. General MacArthur had ruled as pro-consul in this vast, windowless edifice that looked like a bunker. Dr. Hida was emotional as he recalled, "I was at the foot of the great flight of steps wearing an old officer's uniform from the army of a defeated nation. At the top, three American soldiers stood guard. It took a hell of a lot of courage to climb those thirty-odd steps. When I reached the top I couldn't get a single word out. One of the guards was talking to me and all I could hear was 'point, point.' I didn't understand at all. Then, after trying this for a couple of days, I got that he was saying 'appointment.' I looked it up in the dictionary to find the translation and realized it meant a scheduled meeting. The next time I told him I didn't have one, and he told me to scram. So I left. But I had a plan: I would come every day for at least nine days.

"I knew there were three guards, who alternated with one another. In all logic, I would see the first one again. You can usually have a conversation man-to-man by the third meeting—that's just human nature. On my ninth visit the guard recognized me and eventually asked me whom I wanted to see. I took out the notebook where I'd written down my English sentence and did my best to read it out: 'I would like to see a military doctor.' He suggested an arrangement: I couldn't go inside the headquarters, but he could arrange for a doctor to come to the back of the building at lunchtime.

"When I met the doctor I was equipped with my list of questions in English, and we managed to understand each other. The young American doctor was moved by the painfully serious subject. 'I can't answer your questions,' he told me. 'I would say even General MacArthur isn't authorized to do that. This is the direct responsibility of the president of the United States. It's about the damage caused by the atomic bomb. But I understand that you can't just give up on this. I'll arrange for you to meet my supervisor.' And so I managed to meet his supervisor. At last I had an appointment inside the HQ. I arrived on time and was allowed in. The officer, who was a doctor, repeated the fact that only the president of the United States could discuss the bomb. 'I won't even try to pass on your message to the president. If anyone finds out I've talked to you about the nuclear weapon, I'll be punished.'

"We could have, we should have, left it at that, but when I was about to leave, he added, 'One last thing: Your country lost the war, mine won it. I'm a senior officer. An ordinary lieutenant from a foreign army like you has no right to talk to me. Even in the name of justice. Even in the name of humanity. Even if you think you're right, your opinion doesn't matter. It's the people who won the war who dictate the rules. What's fair? Well, power decides that. Power is almighty.' He warned me that the war wasn't over yet and I should be sure to remember: 'Power is almighty.' And I left him on those final words. Oh, I was so angry! Shame on him! As a doctor, he was not only neglecting the lives of the hibakusha, but he also dared to give that contemptible lecture about power! I was disgusted."

Meanwhile, our behavior—a white Westerner with a camera and an old Japanese man talking outside the head office of a large insurance company—had made one of the guards suspicious, and he asked us inside to check our IDs. Dr. Hida was astonished to see what had become of the U.S. forces' old head-quarters. Apparently, some floors had been knocked down to make way for a vast cathedral-like space in high-end materials. We were in the inner sanctum of triumphal capitalism. As we ascended the esca-lators—now escorted by two guards—I tried to imagine how the doctor felt. I cast my mind back to the suffering of the hibakusha in Hiroshima: There was something indecent about introducing these memories into this place. I regretted bringing him here. One of the guards reappeared, accompanied by someone from the insurance company's com-munications department, and he said he couldn't give us permission to use images of their building in our film because it would risk displeasing some of their clients. It was only once I was back home and had done some internet research that I understood why: Among their many clients was Tepco, the very company that manages the site of the Fukushima nuclear plant...

Dr. Hida continued with his story: "That meeting with the American officer opened my eyes—so long as this army from the Allied forces occupied our coun-try, we wouldn't be able to save the irradiated victims or provide them with solutions. The first thing we needed to do was send that army home. But how to go

about it? The Communist Party* was the only political party insisting on the U.S. Army's retreat from
Japanese territory. When I emerged from the American HQ, I went to sign up at the Communist Party's
head office in the Yoyogi neighborhood. It felt like
the only way I could fight my battle. That was in 1948.

"If I was to achieve my mission in the country's
administration at a national level I needed to move to
Tokyo. I arranged to be posted—officially as an internist—to the Kohu Daibyouin in Chiba, a former military psychiatric hospital that had become a national
hospital after the reform. In reality I worked full-
time at the union. Then the hospital director asked
to see me one day, to discuss a very sensitive topic.
So early that evening, I knocked on the door to his
office. He was sitting, and to respect protocol, I had
to stay standing as a sign of respect while I listened to
what he wanted to tell me. To my surprise, he leapt
to his feet, came over to me, went down on his knees,

---

* The Japanese Communist Party was founded in secret in 1922 and was harshly
persecuted by the imperial police. It was the only Japanese political faction to
oppose Japan's involvement in World War II. Legalized in 1945, it committed
to establishing a presence in parliament, and in the early 1950s Stalin inti-
mated that it should fall in line with his insurrectional strategy. This gave the
U.S. Army an excuse for its Red purge, which was intended to push the party
back under cover. To this day, it represents a leading political force in Japan,
a sort of moral safeguard against the conservative unanimism of the rest the
country's political class.

and took my hand. Then he bowed to ask my forgiveness and said, 'What I'm about to say doesn't come from me, the director of this hospital. It's an order that came directly from General MacArthur. I'm just the messenger: *In the name of the minister for health and social affairs…the internist Hida Shuntaro is dismissed as of today's date.*' The notice wasn't signed by the health minister or the hospital director—it really had come from MacArthur. So I replied, 'I don't recall being employed by the Americans. If this notice were from the minister or from you, then my dismissal would be legitimate. I therefore cannot accept it.' And I walked out of his office.

"I imagine the director felt trapped then, because he had to send back a report of what had happened. The hospital couldn't keep me, after directly opposing MacArthur's order, so the minister for health officially dismissed me, and I left the hospital. Then, because I still had to earn a living, I was back looking for work again. But for fear of reprisals, no one wanted to take on a man who'd been fired by MacArthur. The United States wanted to snuff out any claims made by the Japanese people. I'd been identified as someone likely to pit the victims against them—that's exactly why I'd been fired—so I just decided I would never accept the injustice of it, whatever it cost me. Even if my life was threatened. Even if I was thrown into an American prison. And I've never stopped fighting since that day."

The United States had encouraged the creation of "democratization leagues" within unions to counter the influence of the Japanese Communist Party, and the American and Japanese governments had joined forces to undertake a Red purge exactly like the one overseen by Senator McCarthy in the United States. Thousands of Japanese Communist activists lost their jobs as a result of this initiative.

"In 1950, I wound up out of work, on the street and with no money. That's how I met people who'd been fired like me. One of them, a proactive doctor, had gone to live with the most disadvantaged people in a suburb of Tokyo. 'I'm going to come live here,' he'd told them, 'and I'll be your doctor. In exchange, you can find me some premises. I don't have any money to set up an office, but we'll arrange a collection. The funds will help me buy essential equipment.' So the locals financed their own doctor's office. Then he set up a sort of association and gave consultations in exchange for a monthly salary. He was now an employee, and his patients were his employers. It was like a cooperative of medical solidarity. It still exists today and is called Min-Iren."

At the time, consultations were paid for up front, both in this doctor's own office and the others that he went on to set up—the *minshu sinryoosho*, which eventually came together as Min-Iren. The patients didn't need to worry about paying: they paid what they could, when they could, and no demands were made if their payments were late. Min-Iren is now an exemplary medical cooperative that runs several hundred healthcare establishments in Japan, including 150 hospitals, 522 clinics, and many pharmacies. It employs five hundred thousand people, including three thousand doctors and twenty thousand nurses.

"The founder of Min-Iren, as you will have guessed, was a very active member of the Communist Party. He was the one who persuaded me to join the Party. He really insisted, but I said, 'I completely understand your ideology, but I'm an independent person, I don't like taking orders from people further up a hierarchy. I'd likely want to quit very soon.' He told me I would have carte blanche. 'I'll let you do things your way,' he said, 'but I guarantee you'll have to admit you were wrong.' That's how the story started.

"When I was fired, he said, 'What a waste! You hang around doing nothing all day! Stop wavering and do what I said.' The next day he sent someone to see me: the head of the Party's local office. The Party had been thinking of setting up a Min-Iren doctor's office in Suginami for a while. The man arranged to meet me outside a house, a mansion really, part of

In 1953, at age thirty-five, Dr. Hida opened his office in Gyoda.

which would become my office. I would be loaned the entrance hall, the rest room, and the function room. The wealthy owner had been a member of the Communist Party before the war.

"When I started, on April 1, 1950, I was on my own, with the secretary-general of the local section of the Party on one side and a male nurse on the other. To be honest, I didn't know anything about a family doctor's work: with my stethoscope around my neck, I was quite the charlatan, and one day the nurse even gave me a book called *The Novice Doctor's Bible*...He told me to keep it by my desk and consult it if the need arose. He said it would give me useful information depending on the part of the body in question: lungs, liver, stomach, or kidneys. I worked in that office for three years, until the Communist Party's main office decided to send me to set up a new one in the town of Gyoda, farther north, a place with a very conservative population. You'd have thought they were living in feudal times. I was sorry to be leaving my patients after three years, but that's how it was in those days."

Just like in Suginami, the population of Gyoda, which was extremely poor, was suffering the effects of malnutrition and poor sanitary conditions, and this aggravated health problems and promoted epidemics. The fledgling democratization movement allowed doctors to develop a sense of solidarity with laborers, peasant farmers, and other kinds of worker.

"I actually didn't understand what communism was until I joined the Party. Its ideology wasn't accessible to everyone, and before the war 'communist' had been synonymous with 'criminal.' I learned the principle of communism: whether you're talking about politics or economics, there are necessarily two opposing forces. One brings about change and progress, the other tries to hold them back. And the world develops according to that balance. Sometimes one is stronger than the other, and sometimes it's the other way around. The only way you can change the course of events is to inverse the relationship between these forces. If you can get enough people together, you can reverse the trend. If you don't agree with the government's policies, then you need to rally together and reinforce the opposition's influence to change the course of events. I adhere to this philosophy, and that's why I'm still in the Communist Party. Let's be clear about this: so-called communist regimes—whether it's Russia, Vietnam, China, or North Korea—are totally crazy. I completely disapprove of the direction those countries have taken. But I think that, right when it first started, communism helped the Russian people. The wealth gap was erased, and the poor secured the right to education and health care. Then it all went wrong. Stalin lost his way because he became power-hungry before he'd completed his original plans. It's a shame. Not one country has succeeded in putting communist philosophy into practice.

"You know, life's not fair in our society. The poor mostly stay poor. If parents have nothing, they can't pay for their children to go to college, so those children won't have access to well-paid jobs and will stay poor. When it comes to health, patients have no control. Sickness strikes everyone, rich and poor. I can't accept anyone going untreated: everyone should have a right to the same quality of care, that's what I believe."

Hibakusha:
A Triple Sentence

—————

Hiroshima lies 180 kilometers southwest of Tokyo. General Terumoto Mori (1553–1625) founded the city in 1589 by using bridges to link five islands formed by the six branches of the river Ota; hence the name Hiroshima, "wide island." In about 1870, the city spread toward Ujina, with a new port where the imperial army had its headquarters during the Sino-Japanese wars from 1894 to 1895, then the Russo-Japanese wars of 1904–05. In 1940 it had a population of 420,000 inhabitants and about 100,000 soldiers in barracks. Before the atomic explosion, life was good in Hiroshima: It was surrounded by lush green mountains, the sea was at the far end of the delta, and the

Itsukushima Shinto sanctuary with its huge floating torii was on a nearby island...

Then, in a matter of seconds, the city disappeared, razed to the ground, burned down. Nothing of it was left, except for a few vestiges of concrete and other things tortuously afflicted by the extreme heat of the explosion. The battered population had to mourn not only the dead but also every trace of their existence: houses, clothes, photos, furniture, works of art, administrative archives, land registers. Some twenty thousand children were given accommodation outside the city as early as March 1945 in anticipation of the bombings, and many of them ended up with no family. Profoundly traumatized survivors lived like vagrants for months, making shacks out of scraps of wood and corrugated iron. Then they got back on their feet as best they could, scrutinized by the ABCC and the American military police. Dr. Hida was always close at hand, ready to listen to them, for sixty years in some cases.

"The ones who are still alive are old now and their lives look peaceful. It's rare for survivors to be tormented by nightmares—their suffering was a long time ago. Back then you had to work hard to feed a family. We were all so poor. Women did everything they could to hide the fact they were struggling, but they were haunted by memories of the bomb and all those people who died begging for water. They tortured themselves thinking they should have done more to help. They hated being asked about what had happened. Everyone had lost something. Mothers had lost their babies and blamed themselves for failing to save them. A lot of survivors had feelings like that, and no one likes talking about it."

Philippe Pons, a writer and Japan correspondent for *Le Monde* since 1970, was interested in the future of the hibakusha: "After the war there were more and more victims of the bomb, people who couldn't do anything but laboring work. Some of the six thousand orphans were flung straight into the brutal realities of postwar Japan. They became petty criminals, and they were behind a large gang of yakuza in Hiroshima. Prostitutes who'd been irradiated could no longer work for the Japanese, so—with heartbreaking irony—they congregated around the American bases. So many tragic life stories that were described in reports during the 1950s, then in a novel by Mitsuharu Inoue, *Chi no mure* (People of the land).* Inoue was one of the first authors to show that in the years after Japan's defeat, a hierarchy was established in the way irradiated victims were viewed. Descendants of the *burakumin*, communities that had previously been discriminated against, were now even more

---

* A film adaption directed by Kei Kumai, *Apart from Life*, was released in 1970.

socially rejected. After them, right at the bottom of the social scale, were Korean bomb victims."*

Some of the hibakusha had to bear the burden of a new physical appearance: burns on their face or arms, discolored skin, keloids (painful scars that continued to grow) caused by shards of glass projected into their bodies like arrows. Women knew that with these new mutilated and damaged bodies they wouldn't find husbands. Many stayed indoors or took their own lives to avoid braving this handicap. Some people's symptoms appeared only gradually: hair loss or a sharp rise in white blood cells—a forerunner of leukemia. They lived with this terror for decades, like the sword of Damocles hanging over them. And they could tell from the way other people looked at them that they were different. The population equated irradiated survivors with plague victims or lepers. These victims—a minority of more than three hundred thousand people in the 1980s—had to accept their identity as hibakusha.

Masuji Ibuse's 1965 novel *Kuroi ame* (*Black Rain*), which was adapted for the screen by Shohei Imamura in 1989, dramatically depicts the difficulties that hibakusha had in finding marriage partners, because

---

* Philippe Pons, "Des survivants contaminés, indésirables et déshumanisés" (Dehumanized, undesirable, and contaminated survivors), *Le Monde*, July 25, 2005.

potential in-laws were afraid of the effects of radiation on their descendants. Victims of the Fukushima accident are subject to the same prejudices today. They're viewed with suspicion as prospective marriage partners, employees, or students. A mother from Iwaki elaborates: "One of my coworkers came to Iwaki to be safe in a city with less pollution than Fukushima, where she used to live. She had a child in middle school who didn't settle in their new school—it's not easy for teenagers. I don't know what the other kids did, I'm not sure what happened, but they had to leave Iwaki six months after they arrived. Her child felt rejected. They did a lot of thinking, and in spite of everything, they decided to go back to Fukushima, perfectly aware how high the levels of radioactivity are there. We're all victims of the accident, but if people come to our city to escape more contaminated areas, we should welcome them. But are we prepared to do that without any discrimination?"

"Doctor to the hibakusha" is a specialty that had to be invented. But Dr. Hida's work goes beyond the simple act of treating; he sees the longevity of his patients as a pacifist political act: "A lot of survivors fell ill much later, when they thought they'd put it all behind them. It was a double blow. The same scenario may be lying in wait for the people of Fukushima, and that makes

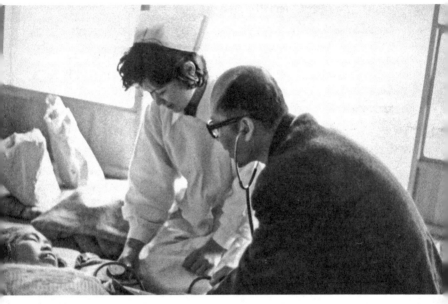

Dr. Hida at the bedside of an irradiated patient, 1963

me sad. Since the end of the war, I've been fighting alongside survivors to defeat the atomic bomb by demonstrating their life force. 'Living a long life in good health' is a victory against the atomic bomb. It's our revenge on the people who dropped it on our heads and set it off to kill us. We must do everything we can to survive. You could say we've won on the day we die of old age.

"The most common health problems are leukemia and other cancers, then diabetes and heart disease. What can we do to avoid them? I've concentrated on one condition each year. After a year working on high blood pressure, I wrote a little pamphlet, which I sold for one hundred yen, in other words nothing. I told all those old people—well, they were barely in their fifties at the time!—to read it carefully. I encouraged them to respect the advice to delay their deaths. I know what these people need more than medical treatment: long-term, personalized care. There are higher risks of health issues for bomb survivors than for other people. Bearing all these factors in mind, I lead them toward as healthy a life as possible to minimize the risks. I doubt anyone but me could do that, because you need to have lived through it to understand what it's like to be irradiated."

Like Dr. Hida, a number of other doctors from Hiroshima have cared for hibakusha over many years to understand the symptoms of irradiation. They had nothing concrete on which to base treatments, they were all starting from scratch. If they made any progress, it was down to intuition and cross-referencing, it was thanks to their stubborn determination, and based on clinical observation. This was how Dr. Shigeto Fumio, director of the A-Bomb Hospital in Hiroshima, established the link between the bomb and leukemia, having noticed the high rates of leukemia among his patients.* These doctors had the courage to go against the position of the Japanese government and the American occupiers, which held that residual radiation levels were too weak to present any sort of danger: "Why do you want the bomb to be the cause of all your diseases?" they asked. "How can you prove it?"

The story of Dr. Philippe-Ignace Semmelweis (1818–65), described by Louis-Ferdinand Céline in his 1924 medical thesis, demonstrated the importance of intuition in medicine and the extraordinary resistance that the academy put up to this discovery. In the nineteenth century a significant number of women died of puerperal fever after giving birth in hospitals. Dr. Semmelweis, an obstetrician in Vienna, noticed that there were more deaths in the maternity unit where there were students. He prepared an anti-

---

* Cf. Kenzaburo Oe, *Hiroshima Notes*, Grove Press, 1996.

septic solution and asked them to wash their hands before touching women during childbirth. Mortality rates went down markedly, confirming his intuition that students were going straight from the dissection room to the labor ward and transmitting bacteria from decomposing bodies to these women, who then died brutally quick deaths.

There was a time when more women died giving birth in hospitals than at home, and yet academies the world over refused to take Semmelweis's discovery into consideration, and it was years before this elementary hygiene measure was eventually adopted into surgical procedures. This was because, as Céline writes, "People kept asking about the 'why' for this measure, it didn't fit with any part of the scientific mindset at the time. It was a pure invention."*

Doctors in Hiroshima and Nagasaki demonstrated their own creativity: they had to invent everything. They were not privy to research at the ABCC, which wasn't interested in their clinical work—a stance that was detrimental to hibakusha. Dr. Hida was well aware that he had no proof to support what he was suggesting, but it was a question of common sense: a bomb that produces such obvious visible effects was very likely to cause terrible invisible ones on the body's cells and internal structures.

---

* Louis-Ferdinand Céline, *Semmelweis (1818–1865)*, Gallimard, 1952.

"The effects that radioactivity had inside the body were invisible. We needed a special approach to demonstrate its consequences, because we were dealing with something that didn't officially exist. If we wanted to prove the point and provide scientific evidence, we had to be really determined. But the people who denied the internal effects of radioactivity couldn't come up with any proof either. No scientific evidence on either side. I could pick a case at random and discuss the symptoms I'd observed, but were the complaints really due to ingested or inhaled radioactivity? Could I demonstrate that scientifically?

"Imagine that a thousand people all have the same symptom. Well, you'd try to find out what they have in common. In the week after the explosion, they were inside the city, in among the ruins. It was established fact. On that basis, we could assume that those people were contaminated by radioactive dust. It's scientifically plausible. But in order to *prove* this theory in every case with no exceptions, you'd have to examine them all and keep medical records. Those documents would then have to be properly analyzed and studied so that official results could be published. If that had been done, those documents would have constituted solid proof to establish the cause of the illness. But while the ABCC was in charge in Japan, it was impossible to publish studies on the subject without being censored. This happened to a

Dr. Hida at the hospital in Saitama that he founded, 2005

lot of doctors in Hiroshima. Young researchers at the university secretly carried out studies, gathering data from their patients, but as soon as they tried to publish them, they were fired."

Sometimes symptoms didn't appear until ten, twenty, or thirty years after the explosion. Over the years, with the help of his patients, Dr. Hida flagged up the condition that some called *bura-bura* with similar symptoms to chronic fatigue syndrome.*

"Patients with *bura-bura* felt so tired and heavy they couldn't even move. But they didn't look sick. Take the example of a farm laborer who was asked to go work in the fields: He set off with his tools fully motivated, but once there he could only keep going for thirty minutes. While his wife worked normally alongside him, he was very weak and covered in sweat. All he could do was go home and rest. His family was worried and said he should see a doctor, but the doctor couldn't find any signs of illness. The wife started losing patience, because her husband wasn't doing anything, even though the doctor assured him he wasn't sick. She complained that he'd gotten lazy since returning from Hiroshima.

"But he wasn't alone in being so exhausted—there

---

* *Bura-bura* is a reference to push puppets, toys with a button on the base that pushes the strings on the articulated puppet figure of, say, a monkey or a giraffe. The figure can be brought to life by pressing on the base, giving it wobbly legs, making it lie down, collapse, or keel to one side or the other.

wcrc other people in their family and among their friends. It was common among victims of the atomic bomb. In fact, it was these families who called this condition *bura-bura*, which describes their arms hanging limply by their sides. Doctors simply recorded it. It was impossible to find a cause if you focused on an isolated case, but if you examined hundreds of victims, you found that sixty in every hundred who'd come to the city after the explosion complained of similar problems. It didn't manifest in the same way for everyone: some experienced it all the time, while others complained of it intermittently. I still sometimes get new patients now, and when I ask them what's wrong, they say they feel heavy. Just staying upright on a chair is unmanageable; they eventually sit on the floor and then lie down. I don't know any disease that produces exhaustion like that.

"Of course, people are tired after spending a whole night playing mah-jongg or a day playing golf—a doctor can easily understand and evaluate that sort of tiredness. But with *bura-bura* syndrome, you really have to know about it to identify it."

The French singer Colette Magny wrote the song "Bura Bura" in 1967 as an homage to people suffering from the syndrome: "Too tired to work, not tired enough to die." Those words encapsulate the hibakusha's inhuman circumstances: a diminished life. Radioactive contamination took hold in the most intimate aspects of their existence, as Dr. Hida describes in the case of Mrs. Kanazawa: "I'd like to tell you about a woman who took her own life without managing to discuss what she was going through. Her suicide devastated me. She was a victim of *bura-bura* syndrome, and it had delayed her marriage. She eventually married at twenty-eight, but she was too physically weak and couldn't reciprocate her husband's enthusiasm when, like any newlywed, he wanted to make love every night. They separated, and she swore to herself she would never remarry.

"She was thirty-four when another man proposed to her. He was a widower, had no children, and was a manager in a big company. He had domestic staff who took care of everything, so she didn't have to do anything and could devote her time to whatever she wanted. She was a very beautiful woman; he was proud of her and took her everywhere—the movies, the theater, trips. Everything changed when she was forty-five. He was nearing fifty, good years for a man. Naturally, he loved her and desired her. Since they'd been together, she'd managed to regain her confidence in herself as a woman and enjoyed a full sex life. Then one evening, just before she reached orgasm, she felt strangely heavy. Obviously, he sensed something and asked her what was going on, but she didn't understand any more than he did. She just said she didn't feel too good, and they left it at that. He let her rest for a few days, but the same thing happened again.

"He recommended a doctor to her—he could afford to see the best doctors at the University of Tokyo—but Mrs. Kanazawa was discreet. She didn't know how to broach the subject. Time passed, and the problem became more and more of a burden to her. Eventually, she heard about me. At the reception desk, she didn't mention that she was a victim of irradiation. She didn't even show them the special health record that radiation victims carry. When she sat down in my office, I expected her to talk about her problem, but we actually just chatted about everything and anything. She expressed herself clearly and she was very beautiful, so I enjoyed her company. She came about once a month, and every time I asked her what was wrong with her, she said she sometimes suddenly felt very heavy just when she least expected it.

"This symptom perfectly corresponded with *burabura*. At least, that's what I suspected it was. So I asked her how she spent her days. She could do the housework and make meals without any trouble; the symptom presented itself only as I've described…but she didn't say so. Then she stopped coming. I sensed that she hadn't been able to tell me the truth. Her last visit had been in late November, and then in February I received a very long letter. It said that by the time I read it she would be dead. She'd decided to tell me in writing what she'd never managed to say to me: in that letter she confided everything I've just told you. I was convinced it was the effect of internal irradiation. I checked with psychologist contacts of mine that there was no known pathology that could produce this sort of effect in a patient. It must have been a manifestation of the illness known as *bura-bura* syndrome, which I know well. In her case sensory stimulation triggered the symptom..."

In 2005 I accompanied Dr. Hida to a meeting of the Shirasagi (White Heron) Association for hibakusha, an organization he ran in Saitama. Some twenty people had gathered in a nondescript little place on a dead-end street near the elevated railroad. The warm welcome given to the doctor allowed me to see him in a new light, part father figure and part gang leader. But what I'd first noticed when I arrived were slightly off-putting scarred faces and surly, desultory body language. Then I gradually started to feel empathy.

We filmed the group for a long time as they arranged a mailing of the association's information sheet. Some wrote addresses, stuck on postage stamps, or noisily thumped-down rubber stamps. Others, in the kitchen, shared memories of the horrors they'd experienced in Hiroshima while they made potato fritters. They were all proud to describe their own experience of the atomic explosion, and I was touched by the freedom, irony, and intelligence in the way they talked about life.

Years later, I came across one of the people who'd been there that day, Michiko Hattori, and he told me his story: "One of my children often had dislocations when he was little. An American doctor said this was because I'd been irradiated, but that was never recognized by the Japanese authorities. He was operated on and hospitalized for four long months at the Toho University Hospital in Tokyo. They told us the dislocations were congenital, even though there was no family precedent. I took him to see several specialists. There must be a link between these dislocations and the fact that I was irradiated, but there was no way to prove it. My son walks with a limp. One of his legs is shorter than the other and very thin. I also took photos of him in the hospital in the hope it would serve as proof someday. I saw quite a few doctors, but it never went anywhere, no one took me seriously.

"In the United States, the daughter of a former military doctor who'd been on the team that developed the atomic bomb also had serious problems with dislocations. The government bought his silence by giving him some real estate and a sum of money. The States could do things like that. In Japan there was nothing to be gained by coming forward as a victim. It was the opposite: people were ashamed of being victims. Do you think I'm making a big fuss about my son who limps because of the atomic bomb? Absolutely not, I do my best to keep it as discreet as possible. I'm convinced his problem is connected to the bomb. I would so love to prove it, if only I could! I would so love to have benefited from compensation for him. My poor son's disabled, but no one wants to recognize the link between his health problem, the atomic bomb, and radioactivity. I think future generations may well be born with this sort of disability."

The third aspect of the hibakusha's triple sentence is this absence of recognition from the state. Not being recognized as a victim amounts to having your very existence denied. Hibakusha came to realize that they were a burden, surplus to requirements.

"We were living reminders of Japan's defeat. After the war, people didn't want to see us or hear us," one of them told me. The hibakusha would have liked to live like everyone else, not needing to seek compensation, but they were weakened and therefore couldn't work so hard, and they were vulnerable to being refused employment. And this was on top of their health problems. Twelve years after the bomb, under pressure from associations for radiation victims, the government finally devised the hibakusha survivor certificate, which proved that those who carried it had been irradiated at Hiroshima or Nagasaki.

With this certificate, the state finally acknowledged the realities of life as a hibakusha.

But being recognized as a victim could also act against them, as one of Dr. Hida's patients, Daigo, explained: "I was given my certificate fifty years after the war. I went to Hiroshima in the two weeks after the bomb. If you have a hibakusha certificate, your children can have problems getting married. So my wife didn't want me to have it. People thought we couldn't have normal children. They hated hibakusha. So we hid!"

I've seen hundreds of archive photos of irradiated Japanese citizens: dead, wounded, burned, charred. When I looked at them, my sense of indecency derived not so much from the horrors depicted as from the absence of humanity. Those people had been reduced to brutalized bodies, objects to be photographed, products of the bomb. I tried to reassure myself by searching through the images for a look or gesture that I could associate with the human world, but found nothing.

Emiko, a woman I met at the Shirasagi Association, could have featured in one of those photos. Her face was scarred where shards of window glass had disfigured her. I was struck by her still-intense bitterness toward the people who'd dropped the bomb sixty years earlier: "At first, when I was younger,

I wanted the Americans to apologize. For them at least to say sorry. I still think that today. *I* wouldn't want to go to the United States. I still feel hate now."

Does time erase memories of suffering? How can I forgive the people who launched the bomb? Should I still condemn its creators? These questions go hand in hand with the status of bomb victim. In the case of atomic bombs, the rift between those for or against a pardon was mostly a schism between Christians and non-Christians (Shintoists, Buddhists, Communists), and between victims from Nagasaki and those from Hiroshima. "Hiroshima is full of resentment, Nagasaki prays," wrote Dr. Takashi Nagai, probably still the most widely known hibakusha.

There's relatively little said about the second bomb, as if the first were a catalyst for the hibakusha's entire experience and all their suffering. On the morning of August 9, 1945, the crew of aircraft bomber B-29 were blessed by the chaplain at the Tinian base in the Mariana Islands before flying out to Nagasaki and, at 10:30, dropping Fat Man, the second atomic bomb. It exploded over the neighborhood around the Urakami church, the largest cathedral in Asia. There were faithful inside praying. Half the Roman Catholic community*—some eight thousand people—were killed instantly, along with sixty thousand others.

Dr. Takashi Nagai became famous in Nagasaki after the publication of *The Bells of Nagasaki*, in which he suggested that the bomb was in fact divine providence, and the human losses sacrifices made to God to cleanse the sins of mankind. It's not hard to see grounds for disagreement with Dr. Hida, who was more aligned with Buddhist thinking. Dr. Nagai (1908–51) had initially been an atheist, but a protracted personal journey had led him to read the Bible. Later he'd discovered Blaise Pascal's *Pensées*, and one sentence had particularly driven his explorations of faith: "There is enough light for those who wish only to see, and enough darkness for those with the opposite disposition." In 1931, during Japan's colonial war in Manchuria, Dr. Nagai had been mobilized and sent to China. On his return, he'd spent time among the city's Christian population and was baptized in 1934 at the age of twenty-six. He became a member of the Society of Saint Vincent de Paul and asked to be called Paul Nagai.

In 1945 he was an assistant professor at Nagasaki's University of Medicine and head of the radiology department. He'd been one of the first doctors in

---

* Southern Japan was evangelized by Jesuit missionaries in the sixteenth century. Catholicism was then banned for two centuries and reauthorized when the country was forcibly opened up to foreigners in 1854. Throughout this period, Japan's Catholics were subjected to discrimination, as the hibakusha would be later.

Japan to use X-rays to diagnose tuberculosis. In 1942 he'd learned that due to his exposure to X-rays, he had a form of leukemia and had only a few years to live. At the time of the explosion, he was only seven hundred meters from the epicenter. Although seriously wounded by shards of glass, he immediately started organizing rescue squads with the university's medical staff. For three months they worked tirelessly, to the point of exhaustion, tending to hundreds of victims in the Mitsuyama valley just outside the city.

Shocked by what he'd seen and angry with himself for not doing more, he went into mourning for six months and sought comfort and respite for his soul in prayer. In 1948 he moved to the Urakami neighborhood, which had been devastated by the bomb. His home was a sort of hermit's shack, four square meters in size, built from the remains of his old house. He called it Nyoko-do, "the house like yourself," after the biblical principle "Love your neighbor as yourself." Succumbing increasingly to his leukemia and permanently bedridden, he painted and wrote poetry, essays, and novels in which he described what he'd witnessed of the suffering caused by the bomb and considered whether there was any meaning to this "holocaust" (to use his word), in which he saw links to Christian martyrdom.

The Bells of Nagasaki was an instant success in Japan and abroad. Visitors from around the world, including the Japanese emperor, came to his bedside. Dr. Nagai had crystallized the hibakusha's suffering by transforming Evil into Good, and with perfect timing, ended the debate: "We deserved it." When he died in 1951, aged forty-three, his funeral was attended by twenty-thousand people. The song of Nagasaki's hibakusha is suffused with his Catholic fervor:

> *The mild night and the moon are reflected*
> *On my fragile home*
> *On pillars*
> *The Virgin Mary, so generous and pure*
> *Comforts us*
> *Encourages us*
> *Oh Nagasaki*
> *Sound the bell of Nagasaki*

There can never be any doubt about Dr. Nagai's faith; but it's legitimate to question the connection some people established between God and the atomic bombs.

On his return from a trip to Nagasaki in 2005, Philippe Pons wrote: "Outside the reconstructed cathedral, there are statues that withstood the explosion with blackish trickles over their faces from radioactive rain. Angels' heads lie on the grass, decapitated by an 'end of the world' that wasn't the result of God's anger but of a manmade decision taken in the name of Good."*

Had the Americans felt invested with some divine right when they dropped those atomic bombs? In any event, they'd overtly put themselves under God's protection. When President Harry Truman announced the bombing of Hiroshima, he said, "We thank God that it [the responsibility of the atom bomb] has come to us, instead of to our enemies; and we pray that He may guide us to use it in His ways and for His purposes."

How can anyone appeal to God about causing death and suffering to hundreds of thousands of people? Surely this reference to God was inappropriate. Having dropped the bombs with the intention of punishing the Japanese, impressing the Russians, and testing their operational efficacy, the Americans were concerned to put an acceptable face on the desolation they'd caused.

Although Dr. Hida was close to communist ideology and opposed to religion, his battles do appear to have been inspired by Buddhist thinking, which advocates compassion and resistance to anything that causes suffering. Unlike Dr. Nagai, Dr. Hida did not believe in redemption through pain. He suggested a peace-

---

* "Nagasaki, la ville catholique atomisée," *Le Monde*, August 8, 2005.

ful revenge on the Americans by putting people front and center in a rehabilitation of positive values: "Living a long life in good health is a victory against the atomic bomb."

Dr. Hida encouraged victims to stand up for themselves. He supported them in claiming their rights, which allowed them to hold their heads high. His work restored some of their humanity.

The more time I spent with him, the more I felt his actions were inspired by religious values from Japanese culture. So I asked him directly if this was the case, and he replied, "I don't have any particular affinities with Buddhism. I like its philosophy, yes, but that's particularly in comparison with Christianity. To Christians, Jesus is everything. 'Jesus said this, Jesus said that'—I just struggle with that concept. I have my own philosophy: every worker should have a life worthy of the name. The minimum wage should allow employees to lead maybe not luxurious lives but acceptable ones. And by acceptable, I don't just mean having enough to eat. A minimum wage should imply a life with cultural elements. We live in a capitalist country where the rich keep getting richer. I don't mind that, so long as the people with the most modest means also have access to a rich cultural life.

"That's the philosophy that drives me forward, it's nothing to do with any religious values such as Buddhism. Japanese philosophy is most likely influenced by Buddhism. Adherents of monotheistic religions can attack people who don't have the same god, whereas Buddhists believe every life is equally valid. An insect has as much right to live as we do. But I've never tried to understand anything beyond that. I regularly visit the cemetery to honor my ancestors, and that's because of my Japanese upbringing, not out of religious conviction. I have no particular thoughts about Buddhism, Shintoism, or Confucianism."

Vocation

Behind a small wrought-iron gate in the Tokyo suburbs stands the modern bungalow where Dr. Hida lived, and some of our interviews were conducted there. In anticipation of our visit, he'd set out some photo albums. One page has a picture of his parents with him as a baby. I asked what sort of child he'd been before he was propelled into his life as doctor to the irradiated.

"I had a head full of dreams, like all children. And they changed all the time. But the person who really captivated me was Dr. Albert Schweitzer, who'd conducted research into infectious diseases in Africa. I'd come across an article about him in a kids' magazine when I was nine. I was struck by his life, his determination, and his dedication. Very few people decide to leave a comfortable existence in their own country to go help the poor in Africa in a completely unfamiliar environment. The article talked about an absolute love for humanity—humanism, if you like. That story is probably what made me want to be a doctor.

"I then read several of Schweitzer's books. I wanted to be someone important to society, and he was a role model for me. I was never sick as a child so I didn't have many opportunities to meet doctors in the flesh, but I knew I had a vocation to save human lives and I knew that choosing this profession would mean taking on a huge responsibility. I also knew it was bound to give me terrific satisfaction.

"My father worked in a bank, and when he was transferred to be manager of the Hiroshima branch, he met my mother, who was from that region. I was born in Hiroshima a year after they were married. My father moved from one branch to another: he was sent pretty much everywhere in Japan on a one- or two-year cycle. We lived in Okinawa, Tokyo, Yokohama, Sakai Osaka. I went to a lot of schools. We moved to Tokyo when I was in ninth grade, and we stayed there.

"I was always in the top three in class. But I don't think I worked very hard to achieve that. I was like any other boy, but the bookish type. I gobbled my way through everything in my father's bookcase and by the last year of elementary school I'd already read all of Natsume Sōseki's and Ryunosuke Akutagawa's works. In middle school I moved on to foreign classics, Tolstoy and Dostoyevsky as well as French literature. I always had a book with me.

"When you're fifteen, sixteen years old, you want to have friends of the opposite sex. In those days, boys didn't spend time around girls like nowadays. I didn't have a sister, so I didn't know anything about girls. I had plenty of female cousins, but I'd never thought of them as women. I was fascinated by the subject of girls and had my own private fantasies, but I was shy and I wanted to overcome this failing. One day, a really good friend took me mountaineering in the Japanese Alps. Mountaineering forces you to face up to things—whichever route you're on, you're totally alone with a heavy backpack. Of course, your friends are there next to you, but they're not going to hold your hand and help you climb. It's a one-on-one battle with the mountain. When you embark on a dangerous route, you're constantly fighting feelings of fear that tie your stomach in knots. I thought this would help me overcome my shyness and I had dreams of difficult climbs with icy stretches where you use pegs to make progress. I wanted those extreme conditions, and I threw myself into them passionately toward the end of my time at middle school."

We were served tea and cookies. There was a natural mood of calm. Dr. Hida was sitting facing a glass door that led out into a little garden, and he seemed to be lost in contemplation. We sat in silence together looking at the garden: It was a small space, two meters deep by ten wide, with a few plants, some rocks surrounded by pebbles, and a Japanese fountain with a thin stream of water. A meter-high bamboo fence screened it from the neighboring house.

"When I had this house built, there was nothing in the garden, it was all lawn. I had a big dog who ran around all over the place. My father came to live with me in his final years, and he took on this garden, which was bigger than it is now, as an indulgence for himself. I went to the Chichibu region with him to choose the pebbles. I wasn't interested in the stones at all, but he chose each one individually and so attentively. After he died, we did some renovations so my son could move in with us. We decided to extend the living space to make room for him, so we ate into the garden a little. At one point I considered getting rid of it altogether. But I like having water around. When I think about difficult things, I can no longer tolerate complete silence. I need sound or something moving. The sound of running water and its gentle movement give me some serenity. So I allow myself this luxury."

The light was fading slowly, and Yuko, the interpreter, asked, "And your family background?" He may well have been planning to say more about this because he picked up the subject again straightaway:

"My father was descended from an old Japanese family. During the Edo period,* Japan was divided into several provinces run by lords, rather like mayors in our present-day municipalities. A member of my family was one of the most eminent of these lords. It must have been very hard making the right decisions in an unstable political climate, just before the Meiji restoration. Despite the difficult situation, my ancestor succeeded in steering his population of laborers and peasants into the new age. He made no significant errors of judgment, and I think he acted in everyone's best interests thanks to his common sense.

"How did he manage to implement his policies in a world whose values had been turned upside down? First, as I see it, he had a geographical advantage: His province was made up of several small clans that lived in the mountains, so external military forces found it hard to get in. My ancestor was descended from a warrior led by General Akechi Mitsuhide, who rebelled against the all-powerful Oda Nobunaga, driving him to suicide during the Honno-ji incident †in June 1582. June 13, 1582, is the anniversary of the death of the first in our bloodline: in the Battle of Yamazaki, which followed the Honno-ji incident, my ancestor's troops were decimated by Hideyoshi's

---

* Also known as the Tokugawa period, which lasted from 1603 to 1867.

† A surprise assault on the Honno-ji Zen temple in Kyoto, where the daimyo Nobunaga was living.

army from Okayama. He lost his life. He must have died in combat, leaving behind his regrets.

"His wife was pregnant, and to ensure her safety, he'd left her and his savings with people he trusted. They set out on foot from the Kiso valley with no fixed destination, and then when they reached the village of Nakatsugawa, they settled. So my family has a five-hundred-year history. Each generation learned from the experiences and errors of the one before. Some made mistakes, others were influenced by third parties and chose the wrong path. But they still managed to maintain the Hida line until today. And that's how each generation learned leadership. Through the centuries, my ancestors passed on their knowledge about leading people toward a peaceful future."

Dr. Hida turned to us with a smile to indicate that he'd finished, but we were still watching him, waiting for more. We were aware that this was an honor.

"My father never understood my passion for medicine," he continued. "Right up to the day he died. And he never told me why. He was an extraordinary man, with a remarkably open mind and, for someone of his generation, an exceptional ability to listen. And yet he was firmly against my studying medicine: It must be the one thing on which he never backed down. He must have had a reason. From my earliest childhood I'd been proud of my family. It had a pleasing harmony

Shuntaro Hida, 1917

to it, and that mattered to me. Family, traditions—
I thought all that was essential! I decided to stifle my
vocation rather than cause a confrontation with my
parents, even though it was torture for me.

"So I went to Waseda University to study architecture, which was what my father wanted. There were
also courses there in applied sciences and physics. At
first, I had absolutely no trouble following classes, but
the further we went the heavier the workload became,
and the further I dropped behind my fellow students.
When I'd finished my second year, in other words halfway through the curriculum, I couldn't keep up the pre-
tense and started skipping classes. I'd never stopped
thinking about medicine, and I knew I wouldn't be
able to make a U-turn once I had my qualification in
architecture, so I needed to do something. This situation pushed me into a deep depression for two years. I
spent all my time reading, then one day I thought: I'm
just shutting myself away in my own cocoon, trying to
put the world to rights with my books and achieving
nothing...I have to do something! To save time—and
I knew my father couldn't object to this—I decided to
stop studying for two or three months to go work in
the countryside. I was confident I was physically fit
enough thanks to the mountaineering."

Dr. Hida's humanity and his empathy for the hibakusha may have their foundations in the difficulties

he had in his teenage years, when he had to make a stand against a father whom he loved and respected. Anyone who has suffered finds it easier to understand someone else's suffering. Do people become doctors because they themselves have needed treatment? During our conversation, he took a pile of photographs from the low table, looked through them slowly, and stopped at one that he then handed to me. It had been taken high up in the mountains, when the doctor must have been about twenty years old. He's in three-quarter profile against a backdrop of snow, with his bamboo ski poles over one shoulder. A shirt, a tartan tie, and big woolen mittens with a snowflake pattern on them. A smiling, tanned face. I passed the photo to Yuko. She looked at it, turned it over, and read out the caption: "Hodaka, 1940."

"I need to rewind a little," Dr. Hida said. "Up in the mountains at Kamikochi, there was a painter called Kojin Kozu whom I would visit whenever I could. He would always set up his easel in the same place, just above the Taisho Pond. Spread before us was a green landscape and mountains as far as the eye could see, but in the picture that he was painting he'd added dashes of bright red among the shades of green. I said, 'I'm surprised you've used red here. Is that something painters do a lot?' And he told me the painting represented his vision of the world and his relationship with humanity. 'Writers express themselves through their books, and painters through their paintings. It could be a poem, a haiku...there are so many ways to express yourself. Whatever the medium, the aim is to express your emotions. There are no rules. There are no wrong answers.'

"He couldn't understand what bothered me. He told me the red was vital for him to express how he felt about this green landscape around Yakedake, near Taisho Pond. I asked him whether he'd always had these feelings and impulses or whether the inspiration had come to him from painting. He'd never thought about this, but felt he'd intuitively learned to express himself thanks to his paintings. And I was struck by that.

"He wanted to know what had brought me there, to such a rural place. I told him I was a student and wanted to make the most of my free time before returning to Tokyo. He said I was lucky I could afford such a luxury, and he was right: my father paid, I just asked and he transferred the money. I told Kozu that my father was a banker, and he said I hadn't yet experienced real life, I was living thanks to my parents, and my existence at the time made no difference to the balance of the world. Then he added that if we're lucky enough to be born, we have to make ourselves useful to society at least once. And I agreed.

"Then he told me about a farm, the Kozu farm, founded by his grandfather. If I ever wanted to prove myself for whatever reason, I should go knock at the door of that farmhouse. The idea appealed to me, and then later, during my depression, when I wanted to do physical work to build myself up morally, I remembered it. I was such an idealist, always lost in my own world, so I'd kept his card. I was very surprised to find that he lived in Tokyo, in a run-down part of the Ikebukuro neighborhood, away from the main roads. He remembered me and didn't seem surprised to see me. When I told him what I was planning, he asked whether I realized how hard farmwork was. I was prepared for it, so he wrote a letter of recommendation, and I went there the very next day.

"When the farm manager had read the letter and taken a good look at me, he said, 'You don't look very strong. Are you sure you can do it? This is tough, physical work. You won't be sitting around in the countryside playing the mandolin and enjoying the fresh air.' I told him I was ready, and he told me I could start in the morning. I stayed at his house that night, and the next morning I went to the farm office. There I learned that everything produced on the farm was bought by the Meiji company, a heavyweight in the dairy industry. The farm's director was in Tokyo on business and would be back the next day. I was given a room in a tourist hostel. There was even a bath full of milk.

"I was able to get an idea of the work on the farm by watching the cows and the workers. It seemed quite tough to me. The day started at four in the morning, when the cows had to be herded out of the cowshed and taken to fenced-off pastures high up in the hills. The cows were placid and followed one another in single file. Then the cowshed had to be cleaned of all the dung. After that you had to fetch the cows down again to milk them. Each worker was responsible for just over twenty cows, and the milking was done by hand: You put a bucket between your knees and pressed your face against the cow's belly. Then you stretched out your arms to reach the teats. You had to know just what to do with your fingers to milk efficiently. Statistically, they knew approximately how much milk each cow yielded. If you did it wrong, you wouldn't get the expected amount. The Kozu farm was renowned for its butter. Quality was more important than quantity. That was a distinctive feature.

"I worked there for six months, long enough to know how to do it well. I'd learned to play piano…I don't know if there's any connection, but anyway I managed to milk big yields. I thought it was very funny: I was better at it than anyone else, even though I had no experience. The old hands were impressed. You had to watch out for the cows' well-being to get them to yield as much milk as possible. It was a really enriching experience.

"I'd made friends with a guy from Hokkaido who was about my age, twenty-one. One day he said he had to go home for personal reasons, and I suggested

I come with him to go skiing in Hokkaido. We spent three days together at a resort called Sugadaira, and we met a group of girls there. In the evening, I told them about our exploits on the farm, and they loved hearing about it. By some stroke of luck, they were students at the specialist medical school in Showa. They told me everything about the curriculum, the entry requirements, and student life. They also explained that vocational colleges had been set up to train future doctors as quickly as possible to send them to the front: short-cut medical training, but with a proper state-approved qualification. As far as they knew, there was a college I could apply to in March that year if I dropped my current studies: the vocational college at the University of Nihon, which had a five-year course famous for its breadth and quality.

"I chose German as my optional subject for the entry exams, in which I came first. I was three years older than the other applicants, who were fresh out of high school, and that's how my medical career started. I was at the theory stage and had still never examined a living person: whether it was anatomy or physiology, it was all just in books. No direct contact with a patient, just learning by heart. As for the teaching staff, I was disappointed with their personalities, they seemed so ordinary for people whose vocation was to pass on their skills. Luckily, they weren't all like that, and there were two who supported me. They both liked the mountains, so we went for three- or four-day hikes in the Japanese Alps. All men are equal in the mountains, so you can appreciate someone for who they are. I often skipped classes to spend time in the mountains.

"One day in 1939, before going to class, a friend took me to see a day nursery near the Sumida River in Tokyo. It was in a neighborhood where there were lots of poor families. A Swedish woman ran the place, and I remember what she said: 'The Japanese have no humanitarian feelings, doctors refuse to treat poor or dirty children. I used to have huge respect for Japan but I'm losing it now.' That experience and those words deeply shocked me and made me all the more determined. I went to find these families to see how I could help them. A friend called Masao Kondo joined me in this work. Our initiative spread quite quickly among the other medical students, and we called ourselves the 'study group for children's health.'

"Eighteen months after the start of this adventure, we were called to a meeting with the minister of education, science, and culture. We thought he wanted to congratulate us, but it was the exact opposite: He ordered us to disband our group immediately, because that sort of thing was very dangerous for the country. Obviously we protested, but it was pointless."

From Medical School to War

────────

After defying his father's wishes, Dr. Hida found himself confronted with the absurdity of military orders. Japan's imperial army wanted to make a soldier of him, while he longed to finish his medical studies—hence his anti-militarism and pacifism.

"I had one year left to do," he told us, "when I was assigned to the army after the college's policies had been scrutinized. Japan was at war, so students were obligated to undertake two hours of military training every week, whatever their specialization. Militarization was infiltrating more and more aspects of Japanese life: the minute a tutor was sick, that class would become a session on handling weapons. Of course, the students weren't happy about this—we wanted to study medicine! When we finished our studies, we'd be sent to the army and we'd have plenty of time to fight then, but this was the only place we could study...

"I was our class representative, so it was my job to go see our superiors. They ruled in my favor twice, but the third time the teaching staff changed their tune. They were appalled by my behavior, particularly as I was a 'brilliant student,' and they predicted a great future for me...if I changed my attitude. They also told me I needed to learn some proper Japanese manners, and there was no better way than to join the army and see how good Japanese men behave. *Then* I could go back to medical school. Basically they ordered me to enlist. It was so easy to manipulate someone's life in those days.

"So I reluctantly enlisted in 1942. I thought life on the army base was ridiculous. To avoid punishments and even more absurd chores, I became an exemplary soldier. I played the game, I was physically strong and became one of the best members of my regiment...until the day when an event changed the course of my life. There was a thick fog that day, and we were enjoying a well-earned morning of rest and recuperation. I was escaping my surroundings by picturing myself in the Japanese Alps, and I'd drifted so deep into this daydream that I didn't notice that an officer had come into the room. All my friends stood to attention, but I didn't, because I didn't even know he was there. I was immediately summoned to the commandant's office, and in front of the officers, asked why I hadn't saluted. If I'd just told the truth, the punishment would probably have been less severe, but I said, 'I think I vaguely heard something about saluting, but the information didn't reach my brain, so my brain didn't tell me to salute, that's all.'

"This was true, but the officers understood it differently: They thought I deliberately hadn't saluted; I'd known I was meant to do it but hadn't. Not saluting an officer is a serious offense. The commandant asked to see my student file, which didn't worry me, because I'd always had good grades. But he didn't get past the first page and the words 'Hida Shuntaro, School of Medicine, University of Nihon' before turning to me and saying, 'If you're studying medicine, what on earth are you doing in the army? The thing we really need at the front is military doctors. What kind of idiot sent you here?' And he said I could return to medical school on the condition that I committed to becoming a professional military doctor. I replied that the reason I wanted to be a doctor was to help children in poor families, not to be a military doctor. 'Our country's at war,' he said. 'You must become a military doctor.' And that's how I was transferred to the military school of medicine.

"And then the army, which had its own plans for me, insisted that I take my medical exams straight-away—I was in my fourth year, so I should have had one year left to go. I should never have passed those exams: I knew nothing about the specializations studied in the last year, things like ophthalmology and dermatology. I didn't even know what those lec-turers looked like. The examiner was as surprised as I was when he was confronted with a candidate he'd never seen in class, even more so when he found out I was in the army. After I'd explained the situation, he said, 'Okay, let's think about this: What sort of questions can you answer?' He was a professor of ophthalmology, so I told him I knew nothing about the subject—apart from the name of one eye com-plaint, trachoma. He asked me to describe it, which I did very briefly. And then he said, 'Well done, you passed.' Incredible, isn't it? I really didn't like it.

"Granted, the army was short of doctors, but they need only have waited a year for me to finish my course. Sadly, they insisted I join up immediately without knowing the basics. Their goal was to have as many supposed medical officers as possible to send to the front, regardless of whether or not we were fully trained. Of course, I was outraged…but what could I do? There was nothing I could do.

"That's actually why I've never trusted the army. The army's a business. Some people choose to become soldiers and draw a salary from the state, and they stay in the army till the end of their lives. They're professional soldiers, businessmen. The army wanted to make a professional soldier of me, but I had personal aims and was looking forward to the end of the war to get home. Obviously, we weren't going to get along…"

Dr. Hida then showed us a photo of himself in a military uniform and cap. He's twenty-five years old, and there's something about his expression that jars with the official image: he's looking straight at the lens and there's a sort of bravado or insolence in his eyes. It's an aspect of his personality that he has learned to keep in check over the years. There was something distant about his eyes now, they had a touch of irony but were always kind.

"I was a child like any other and was absolutely not destined to be a leader. What happened in Hiroshima changed my life. I was confronted with how harsh life can be. The reality of it was beyond me, I couldn't do anything for those people despite my training. Saving people's lives is a doctor's primary vocation, but I hadn't managed to save a single one and started to question my own abilities. Rather than letting it crush me, I learned from this failure just how precious every human life is. But war is, by definition, slaughter. Leaders don't hesitate to risk their soldiers' lives, and they need a lot of them if they're going to win.

"What exactly were we fighting for? Japan wanted what it didn't have: oil. Plus, the country is small, so we were told we needed to conquer other territories to meet the needs of our population. China has vast territories, so Japan wanted to claim some, brutally, by committing massacres. Boosting Japan's material and economic wealth was more important than people's lives. A population will reproduce come what may, there'll never be a shortage of soldiers—that was the thinking at the time. Japan's soldiers had fought a lot of wars since the Meiji era, which was when it started modernization with the restoration of imperial power.

"I was on friendly terms with some other soldiers. When I needed advice or was angry, they would say, 'You always react when you come up against unfair behavior or unacceptable injustice. So even in this hospital, for example, sometimes a high-ranking officer will abuse a nurse and—every time—you're outraged in the name of justice. But have you ever tried to work out what causes all this? It's war, it makes us think of human beings as disposable. There's no justice in war. War is at the root of everything.'"

———

When we'd first met in Hiroshima, Hida had taken us to the medieval castle in the city center. During the

Dr. Hida in Hiroshima, 2005

war it had housed the military command, and he'd gone there the day after the bomb.

"Prisoners of war were kept within the castle's walls, which had been razed to the ground by the explosion. There was an American soldier there, sitting on the ground and tied to a tree, wearing just a pair of shorts; I remember how white his skin was. He was just a kid, barely sixteen or seventeen. Maybe he'd been on one of the bombers, I don't know. He was probably due to be transferred, and he'd been tied up until the whole convoy was ready—well, that was my guess. He was looking at me and I could tell he was thirsty. I took out my knife to cut the ties and released him. I was alone. No one saw. Once he was free, he headed to the castle and came across a group of women who worked as army telephone operators. Why did I free him? Maybe it was instinctive. He was just there in front of me, on his own, unguarded. I freed him but I didn't worry about what would happen to him next, that was his problem, not mine. He was just a kid: American or not, it was all the same to me. Maybe I wouldn't have freed him if he'd been an adult, or if anyone had been watching."

Despite the war, Hida remained true to his commitment to other people. Another episode that took place at the Hiroshima hospital in the months before the bomb relates back to his fascination with Dr. Schweitzer and his fight against leprosy in Gabon.

"The infectious diseases unit was short-staffed. Seven soldiers had come back from the front with leprosy, and being contagious, they couldn't see anyone and were bored. I volunteered and spent a few months with them. I didn't do anything special: for example, they were no longer able to read, so I'd read novels to them in the evenings to raise their spirits a little. Some of them were meant to be transferred to other hospitals on August 6. When the bomb was dropped, they must have been in the train at Hiroshima station. I tried to find out what happened to them, and when I went to the station on August 7, I was told everyone had been killed instantly."

The precise moment the bomb was dropped and exploded comes up again and again in Dr. Hida's accounts of the hibakusha. How did the doctor miraculously survive? There was something irrational about this that intrigued me. As well as the content of his accounts, I wondered about how he shaped them. Had he idealized that moment to make it tolerable?

"In 1944, a year before the explosion, I was posted to Hiroshima's military hospital. I was twenty-seven. At the time, plenty of Japanese were already convinced of the U.S. Army's superior power, and from the start of 1945 most of them began to worry about how the war would end—despite the daily reports of victories broadcast by the government. These obviously deceptive press releases didn't fool anyone: many large Japanese cities had sustained extensive aerial bombing and were now nothing but ruins. In early May, I received instructions from headquarters to build an underground shelter for the hospital near the village of Hesaka, about three kilometers north of Hiroshima. On August 5, I'd finished the work and was about to go home when the duty officer asked me to serve dinner to some senior medical officers who were staying at the hospital. I served them in the X-ray room, where all the windows were covered with black curtains. To take my mind off this irritating chore, I did what everyone else was doing and got drunk on sake. Then, once I could see that the guests were all blind drunk, I lay down on one of the beds in there.

"In the middle of the night, someone shook me awake. It was an old farmer from Hesaka who'd been brought to me by a guard. His granddaughter had just had a heart attack. It was a real emergency, so I needed to get there right away, but I was having a little trouble standing up, so the journey looked problematic. The farmer took me on the pannier rack on his bicycle. My memories of the trip are pretty vague now; I just remember seeing twinkling stars reflected in the Ota River, while I clung to the man's belt to avoid falling off. We eventually reached Hesaka and I was able to treat my patient. I must have examined her, but to be honest, I don't remember it at all. It was too late to go home, so I decided to wait till morning.

"When I woke, my watch said exactly eight o'clock, so I was going to be late for duty whatever I did. I slowly put on my soldier's uniform and stood in the doorway of the house, looking at the sky over Hiroshima. I noticed a plane flying at an altitude of about ten thousand meters. It was like a little silvery dot in the blue sky. No Japanese plane could fly at that sort of altitude, so I immediately knew it was a U.S. aircraft. Hiroshima was used to visits from American B-29 bombers all day, every day, and the inhabitants were starting to think the city would never be bombed. People joked about it and said that the god of Miyajima temple was protecting the city. So I wasn't in the least alarmed by the sight of that plane and went back inside to give the child an injection.

"And that was when there was a searing flash of light. It was eight fifteen. I was protected by the mountains and was seven kilometers from Hiroshima, but I still felt that violent, blinding light. I was in shock. Something extraordinary was happening, something huge, so I didn't move and braced myself for what would come next. The air became so hot I didn't dare touch any part of my body. It was hot, but why? I went over to the child whom I was there to treat and lay down next to her. I was preparing for the worst.

"Then it all happened in a split second and without a sound. Usually there would be a breeze around the house stirring the leaves on the trees, but not one leaf moved that morning. Suddenly the room was engulfed in thick black smoke. The roof was blown off. The child and I were lifted up by the strength of the blast, which reached us with a slight time delay. I could really feel myself flying through the house. Along the way, I saw the ceiling open up before my eyes and the sky appeared, a clear blue sky. I was flung against the far wall and landed up wedged under debris from the roof. It was a typical rural house, with a roof made of straw and mud. We were saved by the joists."

Two Faces of the Atom

June 2013: in the conference room of a Tokyo hotel, the Nihon Hidankyo association's annual meeting for regional representatives brought together tens of thousands of hibakusha. The doctor sat down for dinner with his old friends Sumiteru Taniguchi and Sanao Tsuboi, who still had scars on his face from the explosion. They were happy to see each other and chatted cheerily. Sunao Tsuboi proposed a toast: "May every day be unique and extraordinary! That's my wish. I'd like to have the words 'Happy to have lived his life!' written on my tomb. I'm in good shape. I sometimes teach at Hiroshima University; I talk for an hour and a half about peace and atomic bombs. It's our duty to tell the young about it."

"Yes, it's the old-timers' duty!" Dr. Hida replied. "I wouldn't want to become a boring old man no one wants to listen to anymore. And bearing witness gives us the strength to keep going. In France I took part in a televised debate about nuclear armaments on a show called *Les Dossiers de l'écran*. They had people in favor of them squaring up to people against them. Four against ten. The American pilot who'd dropped the bomb on Hiroshima was there, and he justified what he'd done on that day. He said his unit commander had wanted to name the plane after his mother, Enola Gay. A French viewer came on air live to say he couldn't understand what sort of disturbed state of mind you'd need to be in to give your own mother's name to a machine of war. The former soldier defended his stance pitifully. In the end, I think I won the debate."

Hearing this story, I was suddenly ashamed to be French and admitted as much to the doctor. How could a national TV station have thought for one minute that it would be intelligent and appropriate to bring together the man who had dropped the bomb and someone who'd been a victim of it? Dr. Hida shrugged with a smile that seemed to say "I was expecting it, but I still had to be there to give my evidence."

The hibakusha succeeded in maintaining their joie de vivre despite their ordeals. At the end of the evening, when they'd had plenty of good food, drink, and laughter, they gathered in small groups according to their regions and took turns dancing a farandole around the hall, singing at the tops of their lungs.

Today, most people see the dropping of atomic bombs on Japan as a monstrosity, but in 1945 sensibilities were very different and technological prowess upstaged the humanitarian disaster. Which is why, two days after the explosion, the *Le Monde* newspaper printed these words: "A scientific revolution: The Americans drop their first atomic bomb on Japan." The same day, *Libération*'s headline article said, "This new discovery could change the world as we know it [...] Coal, gas, and electricity will soon be nothing but memories." And on August 9, *France-Soir* felt that "The use of the atomic bomb opens up endless possibilities."

Only Albert Camus raised a conflicting voice in an editorial for the newspaper *Combat* dated August 8, 1945: "The world is what it is, in other words not very much. That is what, since yesterday, we all now know, thanks to the terrific concert that radio, newspapers, and news agencies have just unleashed on the subject of the atomic bomb. In a swirl of enthusiastic commentaries, we are effectively being told that any moderately important city can be completely flattened by a bomb the size of a soccer ball. American, English, and French newspapers effuse with elegant disquisitions about the atomic bomb's future and its past, its inventors, its cost, its pacific vocation and warlike effects, its political consequences and even its own independence. We can summarize our response in one sentence: mechanical civilization has just reached its ultimate level of savagery. In a relatively imminent future, we will have to choose between collective suicide and the intelligent use of scientific breakthroughs. It's legitimate to detect something indecent about celebrating a discovery that is first used to serve the most spectacular destructive fury mankind has demonstrated in centuries."

How to transform the horror of the atomic bomb into something of positive value? How to construct and present the memory of it? The decision to completely rebuild Hiroshima was made in 1947. Two years later Hiroshima was declared the "City of Peace," in keeping with the new Japanese Constitution of November 1946, whose introduction amounts to a pacifist manifesto:

> We, the Japanese people, acting through our duly elected representatives in the National Diet, determined that we shall secure for ourselves and our posterity the fruits of peaceful cooperation with all nations and the blessings of liberty throughout this land, and resolved that never again shall we be

visited with the horrors of war through the action of government, do proclaim that sovereign power resides with the people, and do firmly establish this Constitution [...]

We, the Japanese people, desire peace for all time and are deeply conscious of the high ideals that govern human relations, we are resolved to preserve our security and existence, trusting in the justice and faith of the peace-loving peoples of the world. We would like to occupy a place of honor in international society as it strives for the preservation of peace and the banishment of tyranny and slavery, oppression and intolerance from the face of the earth, with no hope of return.

The only extant vestiges of the martyred city are a building known as The Dome, some 160 meters from the epicenter, and, a little farther out, the Rest House. The Dome, which was built in 1914, is distinctive for its European architecture. A place for promoting and exhibiting aspects of industry and commerce, it was also one of the city's very few concrete buildings. It is now the Hiroshima Peace Memorial and has been a designated UNESCO World Heritage Site since 1996. With its rusted metal dome and its four stories with no windows or floors, it looks to the visitor just like the ruin that it became after the bombing. It is, in fact, the only remnant in the city that evokes the atomic bomb, but it is not the site chosen to mark memories of the cataclysm. Using a symbol of capitalist industry blighted by another symbol of capitalist technology and industry could have sent mixed messages.

The Peace Memorial Park is in the center of Hiroshima between two arms of the river Ota, and it covers some twelve hectares (thirty acres). The park has a central dividing line, with ponds and a well-maintained lawn. At one end is The Dome and at the other a memorial museum designed by Kenzo Tange, an elegant modern building in plain concrete, a long edifice that stands on pilings, like Le Corbusier's Unité d'habitation apartment building in Marseille. Kenzo Tange liked the symbolism and spirituality in Le Corbusier's work. Inside the museum there are photos, scale models, and eyewitness accounts. There is a collection of objects distorted by the heat or the force of the blast, along with personal effects found in the rubble, such as fragments of fabric. It is a harrowing place to visit. In response to a request from the United States, the museum also exhibits documents about and descriptions of atrocities committed by the Japanese army in Asia during World War II.

About halfway along the park's axis, close to a pond, stands the Cenotaph, an inverted U designed by Isamu Noguchi and built by his friend Kenzo Tange in 1952 — Noguchi having distanced himself from the project due to his American Japanese nationality. The monument, which contains the names of 192,000 victims, references Shinto symbolism for protecting the souls of the dead. Inscribed in Japanese are the words "Let all souls here rest in peace; for we shall not repeat the evil." Visitors wait in line in silence to offer their prayers to the victims.

There's no shortage of other monuments dotted around the rest of the park: the Bells of Peace, the Flame of Peace, the Gates of Peace…There's also a Monument to Peace for children that commemorates Sadako Sasaki and all the children who died because of the bomb. Sadako was two years old on August 6, 1945. Suffering from leukemia because of the radiation, she died at the age of twelve. When she was already sick, a friend of hers once brought her a piece of origami and told her a Japanese legend: whoever makes a thousand origami cranes shall have their wish granted. Sadako set to work, hoping the gods would allow her to recover. Before she died, she'd made 644 cranes, using any paper she could find, even down to the labels from medicine bottles. Sadako's story had a profound impact on her school friends, who eventually folded the remaining 356 cranes and collected funds to build a statue to commemorate Sadako and all children affected by the bomb. The statue was unveiled in 1958 and depicts her with her arms raised wide, holding a golden crane above her head. The inscription on the granite pedestal reads:

This is our cry.
This is our prayer.
To build peace in the world.

Since then, children from all over the world have made origami cranes and sent them to Hiroshima. Thousands of them are placed in transparent urns around the statue. Thanks to Sadako, paper cranes have become an international symbol of peace.

On August 6 every year, thousands of people congregate by the Cenotaph for a ceremony honoring the victims. A minute's silence is observed at eight fifteen, then speeches are made in favor of peace and nuclear disarmament. At nightfall, attendees put hundreds of floating lanterns bearing messages into the river beside the Cenotaph. In 1995, Emperor Akihito went to Hiroshima and spent a time of quiet reflection at the Cenotaph. He was the first person to offer official condolences to the victims. But the hibakusha, who'd felt abandoned by the state ever since the disaster, thought this was too little too late.

———

"You're destroying me. You're good for me...You saw nothing at Hiroshima." These famous words from Alain Resnais's film *Hiroshima mon amour* are to some extent inscribed on collective memory. The producer, Anatole Dauman, had specifically chosen Resnais to direct the movie. At a time when French cinema tended to glorify resistance and maintain a silence surrounding the Holocaust, Resnais had made *Night and Fog*. With this next project, he was interested in the lack of awareness. "To forget, you need to remember." When *Hiroshima mon amour* was screened at the 1959 Cannes Film Festival, it was kept out of competition to appease the Americans but was awarded a prize by the press.

When Resnais and his crew arrived in Hiroshima in August 1958, the city was in the throes of reconstruction to a modernist plan, with wide American-style avenues. In April of the same year the Hiroshima Peace Memorial Museum had held an exhibition, Atoms for Peace, dedicated to the civilian applications of nuclear science. How had such an exhibition been allowed to cohabit with the other material in the building? It was because the Americans had plans for Japan.

On December 8, 1953, a year after the United States' occupation of Japan had ended, President Eisenhower made a famous speech to the United Nations, in which he proposed to use nuclear energy for civilian purposes in order to find "the way by which the miraculous inventiveness of man shall not be dedicated to his death, but consecrated to his life." The Americans were offering developed countries the opportunity to

121

benefit from their technology and industrial expertise in nuclear science. Coming as it did during the Cold War, this offer was a way to swell the ranks of the American bloc as it confronted the USSR. And Japan was a strategic element: the Americans would be able to promote pacific uses of atomic power in the country that had been the first victim of the atom bomb.

A lot of money had been invested in the Manhattan Project and the fine-tuning of the atomic bomb. The American state wanted to turn a profit from its breakthroughs by developing a nuclear industry. Private companies such as Westinghouse and General Electric were first in line, and major oil families such as the Rockefellers and Mellons had started investing in nuclear research, anticipating the eventual depletion of oil resources. The most harebrained projects using atomic energy flourished in the United States: urban electricity, digging canals and reservoirs to stock oil, and ships, cars, and planes fueled by atomic generators.

While the United States was establishing its civil nuclear program in Japan, a Japanese fishing boat, the *Lucky Dragon 5*, arrived in Yaizu harbor after being subjected to radioactive fallout from a hydrogen bomb test carried out by the U.S. Army in Bikini Atoll in March 1954. Whitish dust—comprising burned coral and products of nuclear fission—had fallen for hours on end, clinging to clothes, skin, and hair, and covering the entire boat. The twenty-three crew members were suffering from acute radiation sickness, and the radio operator, Aikichi Kuboyama, died seven months later. The boat's cargo of irradiated tuna had been sold, and this spread panic among those who'd eaten it.

The test, which was called Castle Bravo, used a fifteen-megaton bomb—a thousand times more powerful than the Hiroshima bomb. It took place seven meters above the surface of the atoll and created a crater with a two-thousand-meter diameter and a depth of more than seventy meters. The mushroom cloud rose higher than fifty thousand meters in less than ten minutes. Many fishing boats spread over a large area were contaminated, along with engineers and the population of the Marshall Islands. The American government, afraid of a fierce anti-American backlash, negotiated with the Japanese government for the victims and their families to be given swift and substantial compensation. The United States and Japan had agreed that the victims on the *Lucky Dragon 5* would not be granted hibakusha status.

The Japanese had been traumatized by the destruction of Hiroshima and Nagasaki, and anything that remotely referenced nuclear energy terrified them. It was therefore hardly surprising that the *Lucky Dragon 5* incident aroused strong antinuclear sentiments in the population. A campaign spread across the country, and thirty-two million people signed an antinuclear petition. This movement gave rise to the First World Conference against Atomic and Hydrogen Bombs, which was held in Hiroshima in August 1955. September of that year saw the inception of Gensuikyo, the Japan Council against Atomic and Hydrogen Bombs, the largest pacifist movement in Japan, which now comprises several million people from unions, professional organizations, associations representing small- and medium-sized businesses, groups representing Japanese women, and the Japanese Communist Party.

From the start, Gensuikyo has had precise goals: preventing atomic war, completely eliminating atomic weapons, solidarity and support for hibakusha, and informing as much of the public as possible about the effects of the bomb. In 1954, thanks to the momentum created by the Japanese Council, an association was set up for hibakusha, and in 1956 it was made official under the name Nihon Hidankyo. It is the only organization for survivors of Hiroshima and Nagasaki that operates in all forty-seven of Japan's prefectures. In 1999 there were three hundred thousand survivors, and several tens of thousands in Korea and around the world. Nihon Hidankyo had the same objectives as Gensuikyo for abolishing nuclear armaments, but was most intent on securing compensation for victims, recognition of the state's responsibility, and procedures introducing new health measures and protection.

The hibakusha's numerous firsthand accounts gave some meaning to their suffering in a worldwide project that went beyond their national boundaries. They became ambassadors of peace, traveling to every country, telling their stories, and meeting other radiation victims, such as those contaminated by atomic trials in the United States itself. Nihon Hidankyo was nominated for a Nobel Peace Prize in 1985 and 1994, and finally won it in 2024.

"I couldn't conceive of using nuclear energy, whatever the purpose," Dr. Hida said. "Why did the Japanese population end up accepting such a project? Because it didn't know the truth. The victims didn't realize they'd been irradiated. That's why I decided not to join Hidankyo. Their primary objective was to get compensation from the Japanese government. I tried to warn them, to explain that the disastrous effects on the human organism went beyond the external wounds. It wasn't easy because you can see a wound with the naked eye, but not radioactive radiation. The hibakusha didn't get what I was trying to tell them. It wasn't until 1973, twenty-eight years later, that we were able to work together. I'd never stopped supporting hibakusha—I've spent my life treating them—but I still distanced myself slightly from the movement because the people worst affected by irradiation didn't know the truth, they didn't understand. And I didn't want to fight with them.

"Members of Hidankyo were campaigning against nuclear armaments but not against irradiation. Some of them were even very happy to work in the nuclear industry. We couldn't see eye to eye. In the fifties and sixties I fought this battle alone. I did everything in my power as a doctor, but I never went to public anti-nuclear demonstrations. I didn't have time."

Hida's relationship with Gensuikyo was different: "From the start, Gensuikyo condemned the inhumanity of nuclear weapons. Movements against military use of nuclear power have an important influence on international opinion: in fact, they helped change the UN's opinion. Some countries that had been under colonial regimes adhered to Gensuikyo as a reaction to the oppression they'd experienced from their colonizers—many of which had nuclear weapons. So their dreams of independence translated into movements opposed to nuclear armament. But there's a huge gulf between Gensuikyo and the antinuclear movement triggered by Fukushima. This post-Fukushima movement wants nuclear plants to be abandoned in order to preserve human life, whereas Gensuikyo simply condemns the horrors of atomic weapons. The two movements need to walk hand in hand."

The strategies and funds put in place by the United States and Japan were significant; very many hibakusha allowed themselves to be persuaded by the tempting civilian applications of nuclear science. The historians Yuki Tanaka and Peter Kuznick* revealed this little-known aspect of nuclear history in Japan.

Just as antinuclear feelings were gaining traction, one Matsutaro Shokiri came on the scene. He was chosen by the United States government to promote, via a vigorous media campaign, the benefits of using the atom for peaceful purposes. Before World War II, Matsutaro Shoriki had been a highflier in Tokyo's Metropolitan Police Department and had contributed to quashing unions, communist and socialist movements, and all pacifists. He had then overseen the military dictatorship's propaganda. After the war he'd been imprisoned for three years as a war criminal, then eventually released without trial.

Secret files have revealed that the CIA and the Pentagon had given him substantial funding to build his media empire. He was president of the major newspaper *Yomiuri Shimbun* and founded the Nippon Television Network Corporation. In 1955 he was given government posts as chairman of the Japanese Atomic Energy Commission as well as heading up the Science and Technology Agency. He was in contact with the United States Information Agency (USIA)

---

* Yuki Tanaka and Peter Kuznick, "The Atomic Bomb and the 'Peaceful Uses of Nuclear Power,'" *The Asia-Pacific Journal*, vol. IX, issue 18, no. 1, May 2, 2011.

and, from 1955 onward, used the power of his media outlets to promote a large exhibition about the benefits of peaceful nuclear projects.

After six weeks in Tokyo, the exhibition transferred to Hiroshima and then to six more cities during 1956. It showcased pacific applications of nuclear energy such as electricity, cancer treatment, food preservation, and cutting-edge scientific research. American officials chose Hiroshima as a host city for the exhibition, thinking that it would help give nuclear energy a better image. One U.S. congressman even suggested setting up the first Japanese nuclear power station at Kaminoseki, eighty kilometers from Hiroshima. The exhibition drew 110,000 visitors and convinced Hiroshima's city hall members, the prefecture, and the president of the university to throw themselves into the "Atoms for Peace" movement.

Some hibakusha and intellectuals, despite being fervently antinuclear, were influenced by this propaganda. During Hidankyo's 1956 conference, the intellectual Ichiro Moritaki stated that "The one thing we want is for nuclear energy—a source of energy that has brought about destruction and annihilation—to be oriented toward an end point that will bring happiness and prosperity to mankind." This stance was aligned with that of Dr. Takashi Nagaï from Nagasaki, who'd died five years earlier. He had said, "We just never want this tragedy to be repeated. We should use the principles of the atomic bomb and move forward with research into atomic energy so that it contributes to progress in our civilization. A great misfortune will then have been transformed into good fortune. The world will change with the use of atomic energy. If a new world of good fortune can be built, the souls of the countless victims will rest in peace."

This is how Atoms for Peace returned to Hiroshima in 1958 during the large exhibition to celebrate the reconstruction and rebirth of the pulverized city. Some 917,000 people visited thirty-one pavilions. The most-visited pavilion was about space exploration, the second about peaceful uses of atomic energy.

After this campaign, most people in Hiroshima found themselves in a self-contradictory position: they were opposed to nuclear weapons but in favor of nuclear energy being used for civilian purposes — which partly explains why hibakusha organizations such as Hidankyo did not state their opinions after the accident at the Fukushima plant. Japan, which is short of energy sources, had resolutely embarked on a modern industry that it perceived to be clean and safe, forgetting the tragedies of Hiroshima and Nagasaki. In late 1956, President Eisenhower informed the United Nations that the United States had reached agreements with thirty-seven countries to build nuclear reactors, and that he was in negotiations with fourteen more. Japan had bought its first commercial reactor from Great Britain, but soon turned to light water reactors manufactured in the United States. In 1957, it ordered another twenty of them.

The development of the American civilian nuclear program is worth considering in tandem with Eisenhower's vision for a military nuclear complex. When Eisenhower came to office in 1953, there were a thousand atomic bombs on American soil; when he left in 1961, there were twenty-two thousand—the equivalent of 1,360,000 Hiroshima-type bombs. This figure went up to thirty thousand during Kennedy's presidency. And there were at least as many in the USSR.

Kenzaburo Oe wrote in his *Hiroshima Notes* that the sacrifice inflicted on the people of Hiroshima and Nagasaki ensured nations stopped using the bomb and could weather the Cold War with no catastrophes. The horror they experienced protected all of us: we should therefore be grateful to them, which means agreeing to share a part of this burden.

After Hiroshima and Nagasaki, the whole world was haunted by the specter of nuclear war. The Hiroshima bomb not only brought an end to World War II, it also initiated the Cold War and inaugurated the age of atomic tests. Since 1945 there have been 2,404 nuclear tests, 521 of which were atmospheric. The world witnessed one-upmanship in nuclear testing in the USSR and the United States, and then France, Great Britain, China, India...The number of warheads kept on growing; they were counted in the hundreds, and it was said that each one was twenty or forty times more powerful than the Hiroshima bomb, which had single-handedly killed 150,000 people. In 1966, the Soviets' Tsar Bomba test of the most powerful bomb of all time produced an explosion three thousand times greater than at Hiroshima. This frenzy was putting the planet in danger...

From Resnais's *Hiroshima mon amour* in 1959 to Shohei Imamura's *Black Rain* in 1989 via Chris Marker's *La Jetée* (1962), Stanley Kubrick's *Dr. Strangelove* (1964), Peter Watkins's *The War Game* (1965), and Nicholas Meyer's *The Day After* (1983), movies were to some extent contaminated by the ravages caused by the atom bomb, and the distinctive aesthetic of these films eventually left its mark on the collective subconscious. Evocations of a nuclear winter were depressing: people forced to live in atomic shelters because the air was so polluted; radioactive dust blocking sunlight and condemning the earth to constant darkness...There was a sort of fracture between humanity and the world in which we lived, and the very concept of the atomic bomb seemed to have destroyed the world's innocence.

There's a before and an after Hiroshima.

The Years of Truth

Strange as it may seem, the answers to Dr. Hida's questions about irradiation came from the country that had dropped the bomb. In 1975, he went to the United Nations headquarters in New York in his capacity as a member of a Japanese delegation making a first official demand that nuclear arms be abolished worldwide.

"I'd been asked to join the delegation as a representative of the Saitama prefecture. I was very busy at the hospital at the time, but they gave me some time off. I'd made up my mind that if I spoke at the UN, it would be as a Min-Iren doctor and not as a regional representative of the hibakusha. I was there with three fellow doctors: Dr. Taska Masatoshi, who was from Hiroshima and was a driving force in Min-Iren to protect hibakusha; Dr. Tsiba Masako, who had a great many hibakusha among his patients at the hospital in Yoyogi; and Dr. Kobayashi Eiichi, who was from Osaka and had been irradiated in Nagasaki as a student. We reported on the problems associated with *bura-bura* syndrome and internal radiation but had no concrete suggestions to make.

"At the end of the day, the delegates could meet the UN secretary-general, Kurt Waldheim, in person if they wanted to, but I wasn't selected. I particularly wanted to speak with him, so I tried everything and managed to be accepted onto the team as a camera-man. The delegates were arguing in favor of a total worldwide ban on atomic bomb testing. Kurt Wald-heim listened attentively, then promised that their case would be passed to the relevant department.

"That was when I succeeded in speaking to him directly about the hibakusha's suffering and the dif-ficulties experienced by medical teams, who had no available treatments for them. Hence the need to organize a symposium of specialists from all over the world to share their knowledge on the subject. The hibakusha needed international support. But I was staggered by the secretary-general's reply: he said he agreed to take on the case asking to ban tests of atom bombs, but could not under any circumstances con-sent to my request. I asked him why, and he told me that the report on the health-related consequences of the bombs in Hiroshima and Nagasaki had been submitted to the UN by the U.S. and Japanese governments in 1968, seven years before he himself had come to the UN; and that the report revealed that all victims irradiated by the two bombs had died and no other health-related consequences had been recorded in Japan.

"I was devastated by this revelation. The other Japanese delegates at the meeting weren't doctors, but they were all well aware that there were still victims of the bomb alive — and suffering. Everyone was dumbstruck. We asked to see the document, and it was brought to us. The interpreter translated it for us... everything the secretary-general had said was true.

"I remember that report very clearly. It was just after the bomb, at the end of the war, before General MacArthur came to Japan: an American army officer, Thomas Farrell, made a statement at the Hotel Imperial on September 6, 1945. He said he'd received a telephone report from Hiroshima stating that all victims affected by radiation in Hiroshima and Nagasaki were dead. No further consequences of radiation had been observed in the Japanese population. The same information was written in the 1968 UN report. The United States hadn't changed their position in twenty-three years, and that report had never actually been made public in Japan.

"After making this terrible discovery, I wanted to take up the subject again with the secretary-general; unfortunately, he had other engagements. But he allowed me to talk to the man heading up the disarmament program, Arkady Shevchenko. He was a sincere man and listened to me graciously. At no point did he call me a liar or tell me I was wrong. He spoke to me clearly, saying 'You represent Japan, you're a doctor, I don't know what happened, but the truth needs to be known. Go home and come back with concrete data. In the meantime, the UN will undertake an independent inquiry. We'll meet again in a year to determine the truth. If what you're saying is true, I will take responsibility for it. I give you my word that the UN will arrange an international symposium in 1977.' We parted on those words."

During that same trip to the United States, Dr. Hida went to a church near the UN headquarters to attend a conference about the consequences of nuclear testing by the Chinese: "It was free entry, I just gave my name at the door, adding that I'd been a doctor in Hiroshima and a victim of the atomic bomb. One of the organizers came to see me during the conference and asked if I was Dr. Hida from Japan. I told him I was, and he left. I couldn't understand why he'd come to see me. As for the content of the conference,

I didn't understand much, I needed an interpreter. I was about to leave when an organizer came to find me, saying that Professor Sternglass would like to see me. I was very touched: Ernest Sternglass was one of the pioneers in discovering the effects of irradiation, especially in babies. An important aspect of his work had been showing that nuclear fallout caused a greater risk of infantile leukemia, among other things, and this had prompted John F. Kennedy to ban atmospheric nuclear tests.

"Ernest Sternglass had his interpreter with him. I made the most of this by asking the question that had always plagued me: Radiation had killed victims directly exposed to the explosion, but why had people who came to the city after the bomb also fallen ill? They all had symptoms that I simply couldn't explain. I told him that this question had been tormenting me since the day the bomb exploded and in the thirty intervening years. Professor Sternglass told me there were similar cases in the United States: soldiers who'd been involved in nuclear trials had been irradiated directly, or indirectly, in the case of those who came to the site after the explosion. The American government had banned research on the subject and cut off all contact between those soldiers and the outside world. People were getting sick because of residual radioactivity, but that information was confidential.

"Ernest Sternglass believed that all these people were suffering from internal irradiation. It was the first time I heard this term. I asked the interpreter how he would translate it into Japanese. He couldn't find an equivalent. So now I knew: once radioactivity was absorbed by the human body it continued to act on the inside! My theory was confirmed that day.

"At that same conference, Professor Sternglass gave me a copy of his book *Low-Level Radiation*,* which I read on the plane. I was deeply shocked by what I discovered page after page. He talked about numbers of neonatal deaths: a graph showed that there was a global trend for them to decline over the years, except when there were nuclear tests, after which there were spikes. The professor had played an important role in developing the atomic bomb at Westinghouse Electric, a manufacturer of nuclear reactors. Traumatized by the devastation caused by the bombs, he'd alerted the authorities about the health consequences of radioactivity. His warning was very badly received, especially by John Gofman, a famous American scientist.

"Gradually, though, his theory started to convince people. The number of deaths among newborns or children already in poor health had risen. There was also a noticeable effect on academic outcomes: teachers maintained that, based on all these factors, the effects

---

* Ernest Sternglass, *Low-Level Radiation*, Ballantine Books, 1972.

of radiation on intellectual performance should be taken into consideration. Anomalies had been observed in the army: violent behavior had been reported in new recruits born in the months following nuclear trials. Nowadays, everyone in the United States recognizes the impact radioactivity had on health, particularly on psychological development; but at the time, Professor Sternglass was the only person talking about it.

"As soon as I started reading his book, I knew I had to translate it. I saw Professor Sternglass again in Japan and asked him why he'd embarked on the study. He didn't give me a clear answer, but I imagine he felt responsible. He was a scientist, after all, and his life can't always have been easy.

"When there was a serious accident at the Three Mile Island nuclear power plant on March 28, 1979, the professor had been the only person to warn the local mayor of the dangers of radioactivity, strongly recommending that he have children and pregnant women evacuated. But the mayor ignored the danger and waited two or three days before evacuating them—by then it was too late. That episode made Professor Sternglass famous. Until then, neither the U.S. Army nor the head of the electricity company had believed in the danger."

Dr. Hida extended his trip to the United States with a stay in Los Angeles and was invited to give a talk in a small town nearby. As he often did in Japan, he would be telling his story as a survivor—never guessing that most Americans thought their government had been right to drop the bomb on Japan and weren't really interested in hearing the experiences of Japanese survivors.

"The talk was to take place in a church. The organizer, a good Christian, had arranged for me to speak after the service. On my way into the town, a group of five or six young men blocked the road in front of me. I explained that I'd been invited to describe my experiences of the atomic bomb, and they didn't like that at all. In their view, Japan had been the bad guy in that story, and I had no right to show up in their town calling myself a victim. They saw the A-bomb as a sort of punishment for Japan. I explained in my poor English that the Japanese people didn't know about the evils that their country had committed during the war and had gone on to learn a great deal from the United States, especially about democracy. I told them I was there because I believed that the United States, the country of democracy, was ready to hear about the consequences of the bomb. Well, I tried to explain myself as best I could, but they weren't listening. They tried to block the road and threw stones at me—that made me angry, it didn't live up to the ideals of democracy. Then they calmed down and asked me where I would be talking. Oh, so it was in the church? Their attitude toward me changed then and they promised they'd come along.

"I gave the talk twice: the afternoon of that same day and the following morning. The audience—which was mostly women—included students and some older women who were strong believers. So I described my experiences and said the bomb had instantly killed a huge number of people, but was still killing thirty years later, and victims were still in the hospital today because of the radioactivity. Some young women were in tears, and they came to talk to me afterward. They said they hadn't known the truth, they hadn't been told about the cruelty of it. I think they were moved by what I'd said.

"The young men I'd seen the day before came to shake my hand and offer their apologies. They were sorry they'd thought the Japanese deserved to be bombed and regretted believing their government without trying to find the truth for themselves. They were horrified that the bomb had killed women, children, and old people."

On his return to Japan, Hida and some fellow doctors organized an epidemiological study across the whole country, working together with the Min-Iren, Hidankyo, and Gensuikyo organizations. Why were the United States and Japan trying to minimize the number of victims? Perhaps they'd prosaically assumed that the fewer hibakusha were known to be alive, the fewer people they'd have to give financial compensation to...

"Our visits were not necessarily welcomed by the hibakusha. We had to use contacts and spend a lot of time in doctor's offices to meet them. I made notes about everything: their illnesses, repeated hospitalizations, difficulties leading a normal life, and the fact that some of them were still sick. There were four of us doctors working doggedly to put together the case file for the UN and translate it into English. In the space of a few months, we drew up a list of ten thousand victims. I took this series of interviews to the UN in person the following year, 1976. Dr. Kobayashi had done some essential work: thanks to his liaising with the UN, the symposium could go ahead in 1977.

"And so the symposium took place in Tokyo, Hiroshima, and Nagasaki. The conclusions, which were published, contradicted the official report from the U.S. and Japanese governments, and revealed the truth about the hibakusha to the whole world. As for the risks of low-level internal radiation, we weren't even allowed to mention them because of opposition from Japanese doctors influenced by the U.S. That's why there's no article about internal radiation in the symposium's report, 'The real facts of radiation exposure and the current situations of the victims of the atomic bombing.'"*

The official figure that had been provided by Japan and the United States was 64,000 deaths; Dr. Hida and the hibakusha succeeded in making them concede that there had been 140,000. But Japan's government and its medical establishment didn't acknowledge the international symposium.

In the years after this first victory, Dr. Hida demonstrated how frugal the authorities were in giving victims special health certificates and in determining levels of financial support. "They put the beneficiaries into three categories to suit themselves," he told us. "People who'd been less than two kilometers from the epicenter were given monthly compensation, whether or not they were sick. In the second category were people suffering from a particular medical condition from a list drawn up by the state: they received twice the compensation. The third category depended on where people had been in the two weeks after the explosion. It was within a small radius, something like one thousand one hundred meters. At first, it had been a two-thousand-meter radius, but that was too expensive, so they restricted the radius. The state can't admit it doesn't have enough money, so new regulations were agreed with the Americans,

---

* Japan National Preparatory Committee. *Hibaku no Jisso to Hibakusha no Jitsujo 1977* [The real facts of radiation exposure and the current situations of the victims of the atomic bombing 1977], NGO International Symposium on the Damage and Aftereffects of Atomic Bombing, Asahi Evening News, 1978.

further limiting the number of eligible people. And, it goes without saying, none of this had any scientific logic to it."

Victims were screened by an official committee to be deemed eligible for support. In principle, the law that determined whether a hibakusha certificate was awarded applied to all Japanese victims of the A-bomb. First, the state recognized them as victims of irradiation and then made a ruling on their specific health complaint. If a specialist established a connection between radioactivity and the patient's health, the state had to pay the patient an allowance. It was a significant sum, something in the region of 130,000 yen a month. Everyone tried to secure this right: whenever someone was diagnosed with cancer, they immediately sent an application to the government. If the specialist doctor certified that radioactivity was the cause, the case went before a government commission, and if the commission assessed the case as admissible, the patient would be given compensation. But the commission usually rejected cases, claiming they didn't meet the conditions, or that the health complaint wasn't connected to irradiation. The plaintiffs then decided to group together to challenge the rulings and took the case to court. Class actions like this were fought over a period of eight years.

"The first trial in the hibakusha story took place

at the Osaka law courts. The judge had to make a ruling on the ministry's decision to reject a number of cases. I was summoned as an expert witness, and the plaintiffs eventually won the day. That was the first victory, followed by about twenty more. It was one of the times in my life when I was proud of what I'd achieved. I'd given the judge a book as proof of the points I was making. He read the whole thing—what a conscientious man! He felt that the health minister's decision had been based on a theory championed by the United States, which is where the doctor representing the ministry had studied medicine, whereas I was talking about my experiences, about what I'd actually seen. I cited concrete examples: this patient was irradiated on this date; their cancer was diagnosed on this date, sixteen years after the irradiation; then came a detailed description of how their health evolved from when they were diagnosed until their death.

"A book was published featuring all the case files. I sent a copy to Kenzaburo Oe, who wrote an article to help its circulation; his opinion means a lot to me."

When Dr. Hida was asked to speak at the trial, he had to confront opponents who did not always behave with propriety. During the cross-examination, the representative of the opposing party, in other words the state, asked questions intended to discredit his testimony: "Do you have a doctorate in medicine?

What was the subject of your dissertation? Where has your work been published? How many articles?"

In 2001, the Japanese state reevaluated the criteria surrounding the risks of cancer or other health conditions in radiation victims, and this secured almost full guarantees for treatments. Despite such indisputable victories for the other side, the government didn't fundamentally change its position, because it continued to claim there was no internal contamination. "Seventy years after the events, the debate about internal irradiation is far from concluded. And with Fukushima, history's just repeating itself," Dr. Hida said ruefully.

Symptoms of *bura-bura* syndrome were soon identified in the population of the Fukushima region, mainly in the young. Doctors noticed that the white blood cell counts of children in the Tokyo region were subject to substantial variations. Nosebleeds were common. One woman was recorded to be losing her hair. Signs of internal radiation started appearing as early as 2012.

Today, refugees from Fukushima receive compensation that sometimes provokes envy in the host population. Some Japanese even think it unacceptable that they should pay taxes to make payouts to the refugees—if Tepco, the company that manages the Fukushima site, defaults on payments, it's up to the state to make them, using taxpayers' money.

The legal proceedings brought by Fukushima victims against Tepco and the Japanese government followed the same route as those brought by hibakusha in the past: an arm wrestle between the state and ordinary citizens.

Downwind of Power Stations

There's something fascinating about the smoke emitted by nuclear power stations that spreads over the countryside and the shoreline: it's dense, gray and white, unfurling ponderously yet nonchalantly across the sky. People take comfort from the thought that the source of something like this must be under control. Truth be told, they avoid thinking about it to quash their anxiety. The official line is that everything is secure, nothing can go wrong. And yet there's no shortage of examples to disprove that, from Three Mile Island to Fukushima.

Dr. Hida spoke out about all the hypocrisy and the compromises—particularly the international standards for "maximum permissible doses of radiation."

"In the States, I met one of the experts in nuclear research," he told us. "I asked him very simply what this dose equaled, and he said, '...to nothing in terms of public health. It's more about the leeway to keep electricity generating profitable.' It's about financial security. He told me emphatically this was the truth. They know that the amount of radioactivity released is dangerous to public health, but companies overlook plenty of criteria in order to keep their energy production cost-efficient. Our way of life depends on that electricity."

Similarly, Professor Sternglass, whom I filmed in 2005, told me that during the 1980s, employees in a nuclear power station near New York regularly released steam from overheating circuits when the wind was blowing away from where their families lived...

As soon as radiation was known to have harmful effects on health, a threshold was established. Given that high doses were dangerous, it was assumed that there would be a threshold beneath which there was no danger. In other words, no clinical signs, no danger. Some experts stoked controversy by saying that there was no such threshold and that any dose of radiation, however small, represented danger. In Dr. Hida's experience there was no threshold for the carcinogenic and genetic effects.

Safeguarding standards were adopted to protect

the population from the dangers of radiation, and this was very useful for ordinary citizens as well as those who worked in power stations, nuclear plants, or radiography departments in hospitals. In accordance with this notion of a threshold, international organizations agreed on an annual permissible dose of radioactivity for the human body. But in practice, every country adjusted the level; in France, for example, it is one millisievert (mSv) per year. That was also the benchmark in Japan before the Fukushima accident, but due to high ambient levels of radioactivity in the surrounding region, it was revised to twenty mSv/year—equivalent to the maximum level usually allowed for nuclear workers in Japan. This effectively means that the permissible threshold is determined more in relation to political needs than to scientific or medical truths.

The global standard was to a large extent defined by the experiments that the ABCC carried out on hibakusha from Hiroshima and Nagasaki—another reason to be indebted to them! In the 1970s, Professor Sternglass had access to studies drawn up by the ABCC and classified as defense secrets, and he corrected how the effects had, until then, been evaluated by Americans:

The effects observed in people around Hiroshima and Nagasaki were far more significant than they'd thought: The difference between people exposed "just" to internal radiation and those exposed directly to gamma rays from the explosion was negligible. And this was a tragedy. It was Dr. Segi* who realized that not only had people in the suburbs of those cities been affected, but there'd also been a rise in cancer rates across the whole of Japan. The ABCC had ignored how serious the effects of small quantities of radioactivity could be; that wasn't known until the late 1970s, when the book was published.

And they got it wrong with external radiation: A brief explosion is more spectacular than the effects, day after day and week after week, of internal radiation. But paradoxically, in the months after the explosion, free radicals can do more damage to DNA and cell membranes—slowly and progressively—than if they come in massive doses in a violent explosion when they collide and deactivate each other. This was discovered by Dr. Petkau[†] in 1972, thirty years after the first nuclear power plant was set up in Chicago.[‡]

The genetic study carried out by the ABCC showed that radiation had had no hereditary consequences

---

* Dr. Mitsuo Segi and colleagues conducted the first survey of cancer incidence in Miyagi prefecture in the early 1950s, and in 1957 he established the Miyagi cancer registry.

of note on the seventy thousand children examined. Ernest Sternglass contested this study, which did not take into account children who were born or who died immediately after the explosion. He further pointed out that the study's so-called control group, which should have been healthy, had itself been irradiated. Dr. Sternglass speculated that this falsified study had been intended to hide the existence of residual radiation. In fact, the ABCC had always asserted that the fatal effect of radioactivity was limited to the powerful radiation of the explosion itself and covered a radius of "only" one to two kilometers from the epicenter.

"There was definitely an ambition to minimize the effects of internal radiation, because the decision had already been made to build several nuclear reactors,

---

† The action of radiation on human cells was brought to light in 1972 by Abraham Petkau at the Whitshell Nuclear Research Establishment in Canada. He found that with 26 rads/minute (a fast flow), it took a total dose of 3,500 rads to destroy a cell membrane. But at 0.001 rads/minute (slow flow), it took only 0.7 rads to destroy a cell membrane. A mechanism is triggered with low doses: oxygen free radicals (O_2 with a negative electric charge) are produced by the ionizing effects of radiation. The low concentrations of free radicals produced by a slow flow of weak doses have a higher probability of reaching and reacting with cell membranes than the very concentrated free radicals produced by rapid flow doses that very quickly recombine. Furthermore, the membrane's weak positive charge attracts the free radicals from the start of the reaction. To conclude, the weaker and more protracted the dose, the more damaging it is to cells. Cf. Ralph Graeub, *L'Effet Petkau* [*The Petkau Effect*], Éditions d'en bas, 1986.

‡ Interview with Ernest J. Sternglass, London, 2006.

and a lot of money had been invested in uranium in anticipation of exhausting fossil fuels. Meanwhile, the military wanted more bombs, and in order for people to accept the deterrent value of the bomb, they mustn't know that when you dropped one on your enemy, the nuclear fallout would come back in your face and kill your children. Governments don't like admitting that they make mistakes, that they will have to take responsibility for them and pay out huge sums. When the victims of the Nevada trials went to court to ask for compensation, the government refused to hear their case right up until a vote in Congress.

"But it's important to understand that the whole world is full of contaminated people. It's very hard for governments to accept that all the cancers appearing now are due to their refusal to recognize the evidence, to accept the facts."

In Dr. Hida's opinion, health and economics are linked. The talks he gives are very educational, aimed not so much at convincing as raising awareness.

"We wanted to redirect this murderous technology toward generating electricity, without thinking about the possible health risks; we were blinded by the thought of making money. Major Japanese companies such as Mitsui, Mitsubishi, and the like invested in the nuclear industry...until the day a big earthquake struck a region where there was a plant.

They defended themselves by saying that the earthquake and subsequent tsunami were far more significant than anticipated by security protocols, but the real question is, Why did anyone build fifty-three nuclear power plants—especially by the sea—in a country known for its intense seismic activity?

"People and organizations that are focused primarily on profit rely on so-called specialists whom they pay to make it look as if nuclear energy doesn't represent any danger. You should take responsibility for yourself: always be sure you can make your own judgments."

The Fukushima Daiichi Nuclear Power Plant stands on a two-hundred-hectare (five-hundred-acre) site. Originally, the plot was home to a few farmers on poor soil that produced stunted trees. The rugged coastline didn't lend itself to fishing. In 1940, Japan's imperial navy drove out the owners to build a military airfield and used the locals as laborers. In the latter stages of World War II, the airfield served as a training runway for kamikazes and was eventually bombed by an American aircraft carrier. On a small hill sixty meters from the power plant, a memorial stone bears the words "Former Iwaki airfield," taking the name of a town forty kilometers away.

After the war, the land was conceded to a real estate developer who used it as a salt flat and then sold it to Tepco in 1964. When the exact site of the power plant was chosen, a steep, thirty-meter cliff was leveled on the advice of American engineers so that the plant could be built at sea level to facilitate cooling of the Mark 1 reactors, fitted out by General Electric. The reactors' prototype had been designed to propel U.S. war submarines—when it comes to civilian applications of nuclear power, its military uses are never far away.

Mr. Ituka left Futaba, the small town where he grew up that was now next-door to the Fukushima plant, and took refuge in a disused high school on the outskirts of Tokyo, along with nine hundred other people.

"When the power plant was under construction in the late 1960s," Mr. Ituka told me, "we were told again and again that it didn't present any danger. My father used to say, 'If that's so, then why are they building it in a back of beyond place like Fukushima? Wouldn't it be more convenient in Tokyo Bay?' He was worried because he'd really analyzed the subject.

"Our region is poor, there aren't many employment opportunities. To be honest, it was the least alluring place in that part of the country. Then a big company wanted to set up in this remote place: it was great news for the area! No one was sensible enough to think about the possible risks. The village was going to get rich, people would have work, everybody was happy. We didn't know anything about nuclear power stations, and we were blinded by the good it could do us. The Fukushima prefecture also saw only the good side, and so did the local government. Did you know that nearly 90 percent of the state subsidy went to the prefecture? People think we've been getting our hands on big money for years thanks to the plant, and they can't understand why we're asking for compensation now. But that's not true.

"It's a nightmare. Who received the subsidy and why? Did you see how much richer the towns of Koriyama and Aizuwakamatsu have gotten? It makes no sense. The Fukushima prefecture should throw its weight around more to compensate victims of the nuclear accident. But the exact opposite is happening.

"After the accident at the plant the authorities hid the facts. One day there'd be a sluice gate that fails, causing a small leak of radioactive steam, or there'd be a blocked pipe, or, say, a screw that came loose in the pool...But incidents like that never get reported. The nuclear safety commission isn't even informed. It never goes further than Tepco, and they determine in-house how serious something is and decide not to tell anyone. But these allegedly minor incidents can't help causing other, more-serious ones.

"As for the tsunami risk, sure, the plant was originally designed to withstand waves up to fourteen or fifteen meters high. But tsunamis in the region were rarely bigger than fifty centimeters, even after a strong earthquake, and no one could have guessed that one day, a ten-meter-plus tsunami would hit our coastline. So they lowered the height of the seawall...Yes, the accident was caused by a natural disaster, but also by negligence. Okay, so, for example, do you know where the backup electric generator was? In the basement! Even though it really, really needed to be somewhere watertight...But it got flooded by the tsunami and broke down...Another basic mistake. What's the point of a backup battery if it doesn't work when there's an accident?"

In October 2013, Shinzo Abe's government passed a law to ensure that any information liable to compromise the country's security in the fields of defense, diplomacy, and the fight against terrorism should be classified as "specific state secrets." These "state secrets" could include Japan's tensions with China and North Korea and its nuclear security, but also information about the spread of radioactivity. Anyone contravening this law risked five to ten years in prison; it seems likely that the country's media were required to self-censor.

This initiative showed a determination to forcefully turn the page on the Fukushima accident and bring inhabitants and tourists back to the region. Such a decision is reminiscent of the censorship surrounding the atomic bomb that was introduced in Japan by the United States in 1945.

Health and Human Rights

———

Six weeks after the explosion of the Hiroshima bomb, the American occupiers announced there was nothing more to fear. Similarly, a few months after the explosion at the nuclear plant, the Japanese government declared that everything was under control at Fukushima and there was no longer any cause for alarm.

In September 2012 I was in Paris and received a letter from Dr. Hida: "There's currently a propaganda movement throughout Japan orchestrated by the nuclear industry and the government: 'The Fukushima accident is now over and there are no further dangerous effects in the region.' But the majority of people won't be able to return home because of the high levels of radioactive substances in their houses and the environment."

In the first instance, Tepco and the Japanese state sought to play down or cover up incidents and leaks. At the same time, the local prefecture and regional government tried to run life as usual in the contaminated areas as if nothing had happened. The public authorities circulated very appealing images of couples swimming in the ocean with their children, smiling as if this were the best day of their lives—and all just thirty kilometers from the nuclear plant.

There were also photos of children's footraces in the contaminated countryside around Fukushima. It was obscene to use children as a way of persuading adults to return to Fukushima when it was specifically children who would suffer the worst consequences from the risk of contamination. Can people return to Fukushima? Should they stay or leave? That's the terrible dilemma that its inhabitants faced and continue to face.

Dr. Hida was so unique, so courageous; his opinion, his status as a hibakusha, and his experience from sixty years of research gave him a credibility that reassured his audiences.

"What can you do to avoid the effects of internal radiation?" he asked rhetorically. "First, get away from the site of the accident. Most importantly, get children away. Do what you can. Even if it's only from time to time. Children mustn't live permanently in the region. Send them as far away as possible as often as possible—particularly if you live in the Fukushima risk zone demarcated by the government. You're making an irreversible mistake if your children live there full-time. The government should have worked with the local authorities and organized compulsory collective evacuation of children from the start. But they didn't. The members of this government will regret that forever and will be criticized for the rest of their lives."

He also spoke out against alarmist experts who encouraged people to leave the region but offered no concrete solutions: "One specialist speaking on a radio broadcast recommended getting as far as possible from the nuclear plant. What are people supposed to do if they can't follow this advice? Try to imagine evacuating the entire population of Fukushima in one go. Where would you put all those people? There must be one to two million of them. There's nowhere in Japan that could take in so many people overnight: you're being advised to leave but everyone knows there's nowhere for you to go. What would have happened if you'd all followed that advice? What a shambles! A few hundred people can find refuge in other regions without disrupting society. But if five hundred thousand people all moved at the same time, who would be able to take them in?"

After Dr. Hida's talk, a woman asked his advice, because she wasn't able to leave the contaminated zone.

"Sometimes people have no choice but to stay there or go there. Real life isn't so straightforward. So, what criteria should you use to determine whether you should go and live somewhere else? Should everyone automatically leave if the radioactivity level is high? I'm not convinced of that. You might think that all the inhabitants in highly contaminated areas get sick and people who live in barely affected areas are safe and sound; but that's not true. The decision is each of yours to make. If you think you need to take the risk, you can stay home or return home in the full knowledge that your house is very contaminated. If you feel strongly that that's the best option and you accept it, I don't think you should be forced to leave because of radioactivity levels. Personally, I know what I'd do in your situation. On the other hand, I have no idea whether I'd recommend it to someone else."

I was disturbed by his stance on this: from what I'd heard, people needed to do everything they could to get away from the Fukushima plant; that was the only effective way to keep themselves safe. A few days later I asked him to explain his thinking: "Why aren't you encouraging people to leave?"

"When I'm talking to someone who's made the decision to stay, I tell them you can never know for sure what health consequence there will be from living with exposure to radioactivity. So long as she stays there, she'll keep wondering about this. But staying doesn't necessarily mean being contaminated. Huge numbers of people were exposed to radioactivity in Hiroshima, and lots of them went on with their lives without ever getting sick. Someone may be forced to live in an unhealthy environment, and they may worry about their health, and in those circumstances it's important for them to decide how they live their lives. They definitely mustn't withdraw into themselves. They need to reach a decision with their loved ones. By talking it over, they may find they're thinking along the same lines as other people. Going to live somewhere else is hard, you need enough money to move, and you need to find a source of income in another place. In that case, you can choose to stay, to accept the risk. But staying also means standing up to the people who destroyed what life used to be like and pursuing them through the courts to secure compensation."

I wasn't completely persuaded by this. The contamination of the hibakusha was caused by just one thing, but with the Fukushima victims, things were different, because they'd been subjected to daily contamination—both internal and external—for many years. And yet I could see that, over and above purely medical questions, Dr. Hida was keen to boost general well-being by encouraging compassion, equality, and an individual's ability to choose, along with all the values that allow us to flourish and to live as a society.

In this he could be described as a humanist. When he gives his talks and is faced with Japanese audiences who've often grown up in a very hierarchical system, he always tries to rekindle his listeners' confidence by emphasizing each person's uniqueness.

"We need to acknowledge that every life is precious. Taking care of your own individual life inevitably includes concern for your physical health. I'm convinced that a solid education in human rights begins with that, with each person taking responsibility for their own body and their health. We often tell our children that everyone has rights, but the Japanese don't even know what human rights are. If someone tells you, 'You'll never find your exact life anywhere else. No one can replicate it. So look after yourself,' that's easy to understand. Anyone can remember that. With that starting point, everyone would realize how important their life is and wouldn't let anyone else make decisions for them."

The Japanese traditionally favor connections, solidarity, and mutual assistance at the expense of their individual rights, and this lack of awareness about human rights made it easy for politicians and people championing the nuclear industry to exploit them. Dr. Hida encouraged teaching the Japanese about human rights, but first and foremost he wanted to awaken an awareness that's dormant in every one of us: "Talking about human rights in schools or in public meetings

Dr. Hida, aged 99, and Marc Petitjean, 2016

can often feel artificial. The audience thinks human rights are for other people. The best way to make the Japanese understand the importance of human rights is to start by talking about health. Everyone needs to have enough strength to fight, to stay alive. Having lived alongside the hibakusha, I've come to understand this. The first human right is living."

In October 2013, Dr. Hida asked me to meet him on the island of Okinawa, fifteen hundred kilometers south of Tokyo; he was giving a talk there. When his flight was canceled in anticipation of a typhoon, his friends arranged a screening of my film *Atomic Wounds*. We were hosted by a Roman Catholic church in Naha, the Rinjin Kyokai (the "neighbors' church"). The audience of some sixty people were mostly mothers and children, including some refugees from Fukushima. The doctor's story and his commitment moved them, and their reaction made me realize how useful the film was in the context of the Fukushima accident.

In 1972, after twenty-seven years of occupation, the United States returned the island of Okinawa to Japan when a security treaty between the two countries came to an end, but they kept their military sites: 30,000 American soldiers and their families still occupy 20 percent of the territory (in thirty-four bases and fifteen exercise camps). Okinawa served as a support base for the American wars in Korea and Vietnam, and more recently, for the bombings in Afghanistan. The U.S. nationals' cohabitation with the local population has been strained for a long time.*

Demonstrations against the presence of American Osprey planes at Okinawa's air bases have drawn up to a hundred thousand angry people. Ospreys, small planes that take off vertically and have a reputation for unreliability, would allow U.S. forces to rapidly deploy combat forces on the Senkaku Islands, which are a few hundred kilometers away and claimed by China.

Dr. Hida's arrival in Okinawa just after the typhoon coincided with the delivery of these planes at the Futenma base in the middle of Ginowan city. We climbed a hill that overlooked the base, just two hundred meters away, where the locals had built an oval concrete tower as an observatory. Planes and helicopters constantly took off, skimming roof-tops and disturbing the everyday running of nearby schools and hospitals and the university. The doctor sat himself down to watch the new planes arrive. Binoculars were passed from one person to another.

---

* On September 8, 1945, Japan signed the Treaty of San Francisco with the United States and forty-seven allied countries. This treaty marked the completion of the capitulation signed six years earlier, with Japan waiving any claim over its former dominions (the Kuril Islands, Sakhalin, Taiwan, and some Pacific islands) and committing to taking no external military action, permitted only to form a non-nuclear "self-defense" force. When the treaty came into effect on April 28, 1952, Japan regained its political independence, and the American occupation came to an end.

Everyone scanned the sky. I'd thought it would be difficult for him to be confronted with the same army that had dropped the bomb in 1945, but he was more concerned about the future of Japan.

"I'm worried that the U.S. Army is reinforcing its position in Asia and that Japan is more and more involved with the United States. If there's another war, I'm afraid Japan could descend into fascism again—I worry about that a lot. There's talk of changing the constitution so Japan can have an army again, and to justify this change, neighboring countries have been named as potential enemies, the likes of North Korea and perhaps China. This effectively prepares the Japanese people for the idea of war. The government doesn't like the fact that hibakusha talk about the past, nor that pacifists organize demonstrations. It does everything it can to bury the past. If it seems eager to make Japan a hawkish country again, that's because arms sales are a very profitable trade for big companies such as Mitsubishi and Mitsui. The Japanese government has had issues with Japan's image for a long time—it's an economically strong country with no authority on the international stage. People in power in Japan would actually like to be like the Americans."

By establishing a legal framework favorable to the creation of an offensive army, Japan would also be in a position to start rapidly making nuclear weapons.

There are more than one hundred tons of plutonium stored on the sites of nuclear plants that were shut down in 2012: enough to make more than three thousand warheads...

When we left the Futenma air base, the doctor wanted to go to the beach. The shoreline was still more or less inaccessible after the typhoon that had left its mark all over the island: roofs ripped off, overturned boats, stones scattered about. The strong wind made halyards snap against their masts. The beach stretched as far as the eye could see, under a fierce sun. Along the horizon the tropical-blue sky met the turquoise blue of the sea. Dr. Hida, in his short-sleeved white shirt, had kicked off his shoes to walk barefoot in the sand. I watched him head down to the water's edge alone with his walking stick. He stood there motionless, contemplating the view. Then he closed his eyes and spread his arms wide for a long time, as if hugging the world.

ACKNOWLEDGMENTS

The author would like to thank Yuko Hitomi, the interpreter in these interviews, and Sawa Iwasada for her translations, as well as Jean Mouttapa, Mathilde-Mahaut Nobécourt, Yves Lenoir, and Anne Bourguignon.

AUTHOR'S NOTE

This book was first published in France in 2014.

In February 2015, while making a film about geo-political concerns in the South China Sea, I was briefly in Japan and was keen to give Dr. Hida a copy of this book in person. And he himself wanted to write a personal dedication for me in a copy of the book:

I'm grateful to you for informing people in France about my experiences of the atomic bomb in Hiro-shima. I think it's important to tell as many people as possible all over the world about the damage caused by that radioactive energy, the first of its kind for the human race. Radioactivity is a new form of energy and it's terrifying for humankind.

The last time I saw Dr. Hida was in April 2016. I'd been invited to Tokyo to introduce my films about Japan. Yuko, my translator friend, agreed to come with me to Saitama, the suburb where Dr. Hida lived. This time, however, we wouldn't be seeing him in his own home, but in the hospital that he had been instrumental in setting up many years earlier. The roles had been reversed: he was no longer the doctor; he'd become one of patients, a frail, elderly man. We waited for him in a visitors' room, and when he appeared he was supported by a nurse. He dragged his feet and made little twitching movements, frustrated that he couldn't lift his legs to walk. We chatted for a while. He ended the conversation by saying that he had lost interest in life because he was no longer able to work or to continue communicating. He was waiting for the end. A year later, on March 20, 2017, he died at the age of 100—his longevity a robust riposte to the people who'd wanted him dead when they dropped the atomic bomb on Hiroshima in 1945.